...plate her words, Sam tapped his fingers on the seductive curve of his mouth and smiled faintly.

Avra felt helpless to direct her gaze away from the gesture.

"I think you're right," he muttered.

"That's a first."

Any more that she might have said was silenced when his mouth crashed down on hers, and he proceeded to kiss her hungrily. Resisting never occurred to Avra. She was determined to find out whether his build was due to great tailoring or genetics.

Quickly she discovered it was all him. Heatedly she participated in the kiss, caressing his tongue over and under as she moaned unashamedly.

Eventually it was Sam who pulled back, but only briefly. When he spied the wetness on her mouth, he couldn't resist another taste of her.

Faintly, *very* faintly, Avra realized she wasn't refusing him. She didn't want to refuse. Sam realized it, as well. Big hands cupping her delicate face, he drove his tongue deeper, craving m--- of h---.

He ordered his n--- ... ...oking the tips of his thu--- ... ...s. He waited until she b--- ... ...he directed her way ... ...onna have to work on c--- ...g y--- p---ption of me." He left her alone soon after.

Dazedly, Avra stumbled back to her desk and leaned on one corner. It was some time before her breathing slowed.

Books by AlTonya Washington

Kimani Romance

A Lover's Pretense
A Lover's Mask
Pride and Consequence
Rival's Desire
Hudson's Crossing
The Doctor's Private Visit
As Good as the First Time
Every Chance I Get
Private Melody
Pleasure After Hours
Texas Love Song
His Texas Touch

ALTONYA WASHINGTON

has been a published romance novelist of contemporary and historical fiction for eight years. Her novel *Finding Love Again* won the *RT Book Reviews* Reviewer's Choice Award for Best Multicultural Romance 2004. In addition to teaching a community college course entitled *Writing the Romance Novel,* she works as a senior library assistant, resides in North Carolina and is currently working to obtain her master's in library science. Writing as T. Onyx, AlTonya also pens erotic romance. Her latest novel with the Harlequin/Kimani label was the January 2012 title *Pleasure After Hours.* She will release the twelfth installment of her popular Ramsey/Tesano series, *A Lover's Hate,* in 2012.

His TEXAS Touch

AlTonya Washington

HARLEQUIN®

entertain, enrich, inspire™

For my readers
who recall the nighttime soaps of the '80s.

Recycling programs
for this product may
not exist in your area.

ISBN-13: 978-0-373-86269-6

HIS TEXAS TOUCH

Copyright © 2012 by AlTonya Washington

For questions and comments about the quality of this book, please contact us
at Customer_eCare@Harlequin.ca.

www.Harlequin.com

Printed in U.S.A.

Dear Reader,

Thanks for returning to Houston, Texas, where a mystery is about to be solved. When Harlequin Kimani's editors approached me last spring about this project, I was instantly motivated by its possibilities. The chance to craft this story over the course of two books was especially thrilling.

You've already met the devastating Samson Melendez and his stunning counterpart Avra Ross. Now discover how these two balance their competitive streaks and bickering with the chemistry and hunger that has lurked beneath the surface of all that unrest. The *sensual* unrest between Samson and Avra was especially fun to create as I envisioned the take-no-prisoners heroes and strong, outspoken heroines of the nighttime soaps that so many of us enjoyed back in the day. I hope you'll settle in, enjoy this tale and share your thoughts with me: altonya@lovealtonya.com.

Love,

AlTonya

Prologue

Samson Melendez silenced his truck's soft engine and bumped one fist against the black leather braiding that protected the steering wheel. He debated. *Go home, Sam.* Just as his voice of reason sounded, another reminded him that he was a fool to pass on the chance to be alone with her—even if the reason was for something other than what he most wanted from her.

Rolling his eyes then, Sam made his choice. Hell, he rarely listened to his voice of reason anyway. Why pick now to start? he thought. Leaving the sleek Dodge Ram parked at an angle spanning two spaces, he headed toward the high-rise Avra Ross called home.

Avra had arrived at her condo only a few minutes earlier. She hadn't even stepped past the threshold, but stood leaning against the open doorway. Deep in thought, she scraped a glossy, round thumbnail across her chin. She was still doing that when the elevator opened to her private floor.

Samson stepped out into the hallway and saw her there. A lone, heated curse settled to his tongue but made no sound. At that point he knew his earlier concerns from the evening were well-founded. Something was up. The only question now was whether he could get her to tell him what was going on.

Not likely, he thought with a blank look. Chances were he'd have to piss her off and bully it out of her—a thing he dreaded since she thought that was all he was good for. Still, he'd come to know her well since they'd entered each other's lives two years prior, when they began working on advertising for Machine Melendez in the *Ross Review.*

Given that fact, the last thing he wanted to waste time on was discussion about the threat to his family and, quite possibly, her own. There was, in fact, only *one* thing he wanted to spend his time on. His smirk curved a perfectly sculpted mouth provocatively set above a strong, square, dimpled chin. The midnight gaze narrowed wickedly even as he schooled himself. It would be easier to coax her into telling him whatever it was she suspected than getting her to give in to another, more preferable way of spending their time. Maintaining his stance near the elevator, Sam cleared his throat softly at first and then a tad more loudly when she didn't register his presence.

A hard knock in the distance jerked Avra out of her thoughts. She turned around to find Sam Melendez standing just down from her door.

"Damn, you…scared me to death," she muttered,

lashes fluttering in mild relief. "What the hell are you doing here?"

"Told you I was following you from the club," he said, sounding matter-of-fact while pushing his broad frame from the wall.

"Oh." She left him with the simple reply and then walked on into the condo.

"You want to tell me what the devil is wrong with you?" He slammed the door, grimacing then at her thoroughly dazed demeanor.

The harsh sound of the closing door was another effective method of jarring Avra from her heavy thoughts. It did nothing to improve her attitude toward Sam's presence in her house, unfortunately.

"Why the hell are you so interested?"

Her snappish tone did nothing to dissuade him. One wide shoulder rose in a barely there shrug beneath the knit sandstone shirt that complemented his copper skin. "When you get quiet, I get suspicious."

"Well, don't you worry, Sam. You won't hear a peep out of me over the campaign."

"Hell, Avra, you know I'm not here for that."

"Then what are you here for, Sam?"

His lips parted again on the verge of response. Admirably, he caught himself before telling her the truth.

"What happened tonight—Arroyo dead after going after my sister. Do you think it's over?"

Her almond-shaped brown eyes narrowing, Avra regarded the man filling her living room with a mix of curiosity and something else unidentifiable. "No," she admitted simply. Turning to face him more fully, she folded her arms across the front of the gold-tone backless silk number she'd worn for the engagement party.

"I think Carson Arroyo *Holloway* was a scapegoat," she said, referring to John Holloway's son. John Holloway was a former Melendez employee who died under suspicious circumstances.

"Why?" Sam breathed, selecting that moment to move farther into the room.

Her gaze wavered. "Something that his mother said to me," she muttered and then shook her head. "It's crazy anyway—the woman was probably just trying to get me out of her house."

"Humph. I can't imagine why…"

Avra pursed her lips for a few seconds. "And I wish you'd do the same." Gathering the chic folds of her dress, she made a move for the door.

"Hey?" Sam's voice was hushed then. He caught her arm, covered by the tight sleeve of the frock that hugged her willowy form. "I'm sorry," he said, dropping her arm after giving it a slight squeeze. "Talk to me, please."

For Avra just then, talking or even breathing, for that matter, was impossible. Subtly, she massaged her arm, hoping that he hadn't noticed how his touch had affected her.

Sam kept all emotion out of his expression. Of course he had noticed her reaction.

Coolly, Avra left his side.

"I really need for you to tell me what you think about this. Will you do that?" His very deep voice was most coaxing in its softness.

Silently, Avra admitted that she needed the venting outlet. "When Khouri made the connections between Carson Arroyo and John Holloway, I went to see Holloway's widow, Vita Arroyo. She told me to check

Wade's notes." Hugging herself, Avra walked the room. "According to her, they contained information—*truths* absent from his final story on her husband's death."

Sam walked the room as well, thinking. "Did you find anything?"

"Yeah." Avra's words carried on a light laugh. "I've been through the stuff four times already. Only problem is, none of it makes sense."

"You sure you've got it all? All of his notes?"

"Positive." She slapped her hands to her sides. "Wade used to joke that he spent more time at the office than at home. He tended to keep his most important stuff at Ross. Besides, we'd have heard about it if the police found something after Wade…died."

Regardless, Sam made a mental note to ask Chief of Detectives Bradley Crest to confirm that. He studied Avra more closely then. She looked dead on her feet, but he knew she'd admit to no weakness—not in *his* presence anyway.

"Maybe that's all there is." He took the other side of the argument then. "Maybe the whole thing really *does* end with Arroyo."

Avra was already shaking her head in disagreement.

"Why the hell not?" Sam harbored the same dismal prediction as Avra but wanted to hear her thoughts.

"Carson went to Setha not just because she was your dad's *prize* but because she was listening to him. This was about his father's pride and his mother's dignity. That's what he told her." Again, Avra began to nudge her chin with her thumbnail. "He wanted her to know something so why didn't he just tell her…?" She sighed the words almost to herself.

"Because he was an idiot?" Sam suggested.

Avra made a face, but she couldn't completely dismiss the idea. "Dammit," she groaned, dropping to the gray suede settee in the corner.

Sam watched her cover her face with her hands. The last thing he wanted was to leave but it was the only thing to do. They rarely went long without breaking into full argument. Their current chat had already lasted fifteen minutes—well beyond the limit.

Avra raised her head when she heard him move. "You're leaving?" She pressed her lips together, instantly regretting the question.

"You're beat." He eased a hand into a trouser pocket. "It's been a long night. You should be goin' to bed anyway."

Avra straightened, holding her hands clasped primly in her lap. "I'm surprised you're not making a move or comment about joining me there."

Go, Sam, he silently urged himself but couldn't resist the opportunity to spar with her just a little longer. "Don't worry." He walked over to lean against the settee where she relaxed. "You'll have me there," he promised.

She rolled her eyes. "You're a jackass."

"And you're the loveliest thing I've ever seen." He could've laughed when stunned amazement crossed her coffee-brown face. Never had he complimented her so seriously without the teasing element that usually accompanied his words. Slowly, he leaned in, caressing her oval face with nothing more than the strength of his pitch stare.

"I'd like very much to have you in my bed…" He cast a cool, meaningful look over the chair she occupied. "Or anywhere else."

She swallowed. Her wide eyes were riveted on his alluring face. "Would you leave me alone, then?"

Rising to his towering height, he offered a casual shrug. "Depends on how good you are."

Don't hit him, she told herself and almost broke the skin in her palms when she drew fists.

"Night, Av." He brushed his knuckles across her jaw and then walked out the door.

Chapter 1

"You're crazy if you think I'm just gonna let you drive home after you almost fainted right here in front of me and Brad." Samson's face was a picture of exasperation.

Danilo Melendez, owner of the auto-parts-and-accessories giant Machine Melendez, spat a curse in his native tongue. "Bradley saw no need to call the paramedics before he left. You, however, are acting like a mother hen and I'm fine!"

"Pop, you almost—"

"I'm *fine*."

Raising both hands in a defensive gesture, Sam stifled his reference to his father's reaction. "Maybe you'd like to tell me what's so special about Martino Viejo?"

Dan's expression appeared vicious as he observed his eldest son. "Have you no respect for the dead?"

"Pop, you know that's not—"

"I won't have you question my concern for another human being—an employee at that. Am I understood?"

Sam looked down at the invisible pattern he traced into the top of his pine desk. "Who was he, Pop?" Sam rolled his eyes as Danilo began to rattle off a profile that he himself could have gotten from the Melendez HR department.

Following the brief rundown into Martino Viejo's career with Machine Melendez, Dan bade his son a good-afternoon and made a hasty departure from the ranch. Sam made no argument and simply placed a call to the home of his assistant, June Elliott.

"Did you know him?" Sam was asking once he'd greeted the woman and engaged in a few moments of idle chatter. Sam couldn't decide whether he was pleased to have the information or peeved over the fact that the recent murder victim had such an impressive employment reputation and had flown completely below his radar.

"Sounds like he was a golden boy." Sam settled back into his desk chair when June took the time to breathe amid her rave review.

"Well, the community-relations department was very lucky to have him. All the programs he helped implement…" She sighed. "He did such fine work helping to acclimate MM employees who were also new to the country. He was even instrumental in working with area organizations where focus was on single moms— educating them, preparing them for the workforce, providing child care…"

"Hell." Sam propped one elbow on the desk chair and massaged his forehead. "June—he's dead."

"What?" The woman's already soft voice had taken

on an even softer current. "Was this connected to all the others…? Of course it was," she answered herself.

Sam's expression remained grim but he appreciated his assistant's quick mind.

"What's happening, Sam? Are we going to have to dismiss all of our immigrant workers in order to protect them?"

"I don't think we'll have to go that far, June." *At least I hope we won't.* Sam groaned inwardly. "Can you get me the names of all the newest immigrant employees?"

"I'll get right on it."

"And, June? Keep as much of a lid on this as you can, all right?"

"I understand." June's words came through the line following a brief silence.

"I'm sure the cops'll be round there soon enough. With any luck we'll have the chance to formally address the crowd before that."

"Does your father know?"

"He does. He's not a happy man." *Or a well man.* Sam made yet another silent observation but shook it off. "I appreciate this, June."

"Take care, Sam."

Once the call with June ended, Sam went right ahead and made contact with his brothers. During the conference call with Paolo and Lugo Melendez, he broke the news about Martino Viejo.

"Does Pop know?" Lugo asked.

"Yeah…" Sam swiveled his chair to take in the massive rear expanse of his ranch several miles outside Houston. "He wouldn't even let me talk to him about it. We need to check out this Viejo—beyond his job responsibilities. Maybe everything Pop wouldn't tell me is wrapped up in this guy."

"You think it's wise to go behind Pop's back on this, Sam?" Paolo decided to play devil's advocate.

Sam had no desire to tangle with Danilo. "The cops are damn well gonna find somethin'. Pop knows it. I could see it on his face when Brad told us about Viejo. If all this could damage Pop or the business, we need to do all we can to get ahead of it."

"So what's our next move?" Lugo asked.

"I've got June pullin' all the files for the new immigrant employees. Maybe we can find some kind of connection the cops haven't stumbled onto yet."

"They're not idiots, Sam." Again Paolo played the advocate. "They already found out all the vics shared the same address."

"An address nobody can find," Lugo reminded his big brother.

"It's the only real clue they have. I still hope it'll lead somewhere—pun intended," Sam said.

Lugo sighed. "I pray it's anywhere except back to us."

"Amen," Paolo muttered.

"Chances are it'll *all* lead back to us." Sam took his turn at playing devil's advocate.

"What are you sayin'?"

"You know exactly what, Pow. Papa didn't make his money by bein' Texas's most upstanding citizen. We all know he's got skeletons in his closet."

"Then what do we do when it leads back to us?" Lugo queried.

"Pray." Sam's voice sounded monotone and grim. "Pray it doesn't ruin us all."

* * *

Paul Tristam entered his boss's office carefully, as if he expected something to be thrown at his head. Avra had been even more demanding than usual. The funny thing was he didn't think her mood had anything to do with the *Ross Review*.

He'd brought in a tray laden with her favorite tea and Danish. His plan was to relax her while trying to probe into what was going on with her. From the corner of his eye, he saw her across the room on the sofa. Papers of all shapes, sizes and colors were spread about her. His voice of reason told him to set the tray down and go. He only half listened. He set down the tray and then crossed the room to her.

"Avra?"

"Hmm…"

Encouraged by the absent reply, Paul expelled the breath he'd been holding. "Need help?"

"Yeah." She shoved aside a page and dragged all ten fingers through the hoard of short, unruly onyx curls atop her head. "'Cause I must be out of my mind wastin' so much time on this mess." For good measure she swiped a few papers from the coffee table.

"I'm sorry." She groaned the words while holding her head in her hands.

A frown crossed Paul's sun-kissed features. Now he knew for sure that something heavy was going on.

"Avra—"

"Thanks for the tea, Paul. Why don't you go ahead and take off for the night?"

"Avra, are you sure everything's all right?"

She had to laugh, knowing she was making her assistant more nervous than usual.

"I promise everything's fine. I'm just trying to prove something to myself." She tugged on the cuff of her pin-striped shirt and cast a woeful look toward the strewn papers. "I'm pretty sure it's a lost cause."

"And it's something you need to handle alone."

"Yeah." She nodded and looked up at him with a weary smile.

Paul reached out to squeeze her shoulder. "I'll leave you to it, then."

"Thanks, hon." She patted the hand on her shoulder.

Alone in her office once more, Avra left the whirlwind of papers and went to help herself to a cup of the fragrant tea. There she debated over taking her own advice.

She brought the mug to her mouth but didn't sip. Instead she studied the mess she'd made in the office living area. Huffing, she set down the cup and went to tidy up. While gathering papers, she took another look at the oddly shaped page that had warranted a closer glance. Actually, it was a number scrawled between two sentences: 14918.

"What the hell are you?" Avra tried to make sense of the numbers again, thinking that they had something to do with the sentences they had been written between.

Unfortunately it seemed that the note was written as an afterthought. It had nothing to do with the paragraph that was part of the story on the John Holloway suicide. Sitting cross-legged in the middle of the papers, she thought about what she'd told Paul about it all being a lost cause.

"14918." She muttered the numbers again before slapping the page to her thigh. "Dammit to hell," she cursed, at last completely discouraged.

* * *

"Carson always suspected there was someone else on this besides him. I should have listened to him." Shane Arroyo said his words tightly into the receiver.

"This was important." The voice on the other end of the phone line sounded grated, crackling through a poor connection. "You know as well as anyone that your brother was…disturbed."

"And now he's dead."

"We're sorry, Shane, but this is bigger than all of us."

"Would you have taken my brother out had the cops not beat you to it?"

"I know you're on the edge, Shane." The voice sounded soothing, patient. "It couldn't have been easy having to ID Carson's body, so I'll just forget your implications."

Shane's mouth tightened.

"Your brother didn't die for nothing. The Melendezes will pay for what they did to your family—for what they've done to so many families."

"You'll have as much to lose as the Melendezes when all of this comes out."

"But it *still* must come out." The voice acknowledged Shane's prediction. "It's gone on too long and Dan's making no move to stop it."

"But his sons—"

"I can't risk them moving in and playing heroes. That's not in the plan and would *not* be in our best interest. The timetable will have to be upped in light of your brother's passing. Do you understand?"

Shane nodded before offering verbal confirmation. "I understand."

The call ended shortly afterward.

* * *

"Sorry, Daddy," Avra was saying when she walked into Basil Ross's office after applying a quick knock to the door. "Miss Doris wasn't at her desk." She cited the man's assistant, Doris Shipman.

"Come on in here, miss." Basil's affectionate name for his eldest child seemed to vibrate in the spacious room with its rich maple paneling, plush carpeting and floor-to-ceiling windows. He met Avra in the middle of the office where he plied her with a kiss, hug and his own apology.

Surprise filtered through her vibrant brown eyes. "Dad?"

Basil tucked her into his side and squeezed. "I've been pretty closed off for a while."

"Well, a lot's happened." It was the opening she'd been hoping for. "Some good." She made a pretense of straightening her father's tie. "Khouri's getting married."

A broad grin illuminated Basil's handsome face. "I can't tell you how pleased I am by that and by the girl he's chosen."

"Yeah, the weirdo finally lucked out. Setha's a real catch." Avra smiled over her combination playful insult and genuine compliment. Still, the ease of her expression began to show signs of weariness.

"There's been a lot of the not so good, too." She tugged Basil with her to lean against the edge of the desk. "These murders… I know it has to hurt seeing such a good friend dealing with drama like this."

Basil left the desk at his daughter's mention of the murders targeting the employees of Machine Melendez, the company founded by one of his oldest friends.

Avra watched her father pacing the room and she knew where his mind was. Good. She wanted to keep it there.

"You'll be happy to know David and Noah are taking your suggestion—to follow the money," Avra tacked on when Basil looked her way. "They might break this thing before the police." She laughed slightly referring to the *Ross Review* reporters assigned to the MM murders story.

"Have they found anything?" Basil watched his daughter closely.

"No." She focused on one of the small lavender buttons lining the front of her cap-sleeved blouse. "They've got lots of loose pieces, though. With any luck they'll put 'em together soon enough." She let her eyes drift downward then. "I've been putting together a few links of my own." She noticed that her father had returned to his pacing. "I've been going through Wade's old notes."

The pacing stopped.

"Whatever for?" He sounded incredulous.

"I think maybe Carson Arroyo had gripes with the Melendezes *and* the Rosses. Whatever it was, I'm betting it had something to do with his dad's so-called suicide. Wade was working on that story in conjunction with John Holloway's obit just before he died."

Basil shook his head, obviously confused.

"Carson Arroyo was John Holloway's son. Holloway was the Melendez employee who apparently killed himself after being fired."

Basil returned to his seat, slowly easing down to the corner. "How do you know this?"

"Actually, it was Khouri and Setha who made the

connection." Avra faced her dad across the desk. She waited for the man's reaction.

"Do the police know?"

She'd found what she'd come in search of. "It all came out when Carson was killed." She nodded. "Maybe the cops can start putting it all together. In the meantime—" she slid off the desk and tugged on the hem of the satin blouse hanging outside her slacks "—I'm gonna do my part and dig some more. Maybe I can find a key to this mess."

"I don't want you involved." The tightness of Basil's voice matched his expression to perfection. "You have your own work to see to."

"Oh, Daddy, it won't interfere—"

"I said stay out of it."

"Why?" Ever outspoken, she voiced the query with a frown.

Basil leaned forward. "Because I said so."

"Dad."

"You're skating on the thinnest piece of ice now, miss."

Understanding the warning, Avra barely nodded. She left the office soon after.

It went without saying that Avra was a million miles away in thought when she returned to her office. She muttered below her breath, talking about what she suspected and what she'd uncovered.

Her thumbnail was raking her chin when she strolled through her door, never noticing Samson Melendez sitting behind her desk. She was standing before him on the other side of the cluttered oak top, observing him blankly for several seconds before tuning in to what was really going on.

Sam hid his smile, fingers laced in his lap while he reared back in her chair and watched the absent look on her face change into one of scathing speculation.

"Afternoon," he greeted before she could open her mouth to blast him.

"What are you doing in here?" She looked back quickly to check on the notes she'd recovered from Wade's. They appeared to be untouched. Propping one hand to her hip, she fixed Sam with an expectant stare.

Sam, however, was in no hurry to explain, happy to keep her standing there for his appraisal. Of course when Samson Melendez appraised, a woman was left with no doubts as to what he was doing. Sam's usual "appraisal," however, was most often a purely physical observation of the woman he intended on taking to bed. Rarely did those observations involve emotional attachment.

Sam recognized it, though. As he observed the tall, dark chocolate beauty before the desk, he knew that emotions had definitely attached themselves. His constant appraisal of Avra Ross had finally carried things to a purely irresistible level. Not until she called—er—*yelled* his name, did he blink. Smoothly, he recalled his real reason for dropping by that afternoon.

"Kemah trip's been scheduled. We should discuss the itinerary." Sam referred to the scouting trip to locations for new MM ads in the *Ross Review*.

Avra lifted her hands briefly and let them hit her thighs with a soft clap. "Is your wireless service down, Sam? A call, email or text would've been just fine for this talk—better, actually."

"Why better?" Sam grimaced, unaware that he was doing so.

Avra watched him as though he were losing his mind in front of her. "Samson, if somebody was using our names in the same sentence, chances were they'd be recapping a fight."

Laughter roused hearty and long from Sam then. Avra bristled, feeling herself react to the sound in a way that wasn't altogether unpleasant. When he stood behind her desk, she covertly appraised the stunning breadth of him. She wondered, as she often did, whether he was really that...massive. Perhaps it was merely a trick of finely crafted clothing, she thought eyeing the dark olive three-piece.

She'd collected herself and smothered her admiration by the time he stood before her.

"We leave in three days," he was saying.

"What about the wedding?"

"We'll be back in plenty of time." He gave a quick, light shake of his head. "Bride and groom want this thing in the bag. Least we can do since they worked so hard to take care of what we couldn't."

"You know, one of my staff could give the okay on this location stuff just as well as I can."

"Not good enough."

"Look, Sam—"

"Come with me or the agreement's null."

Her eyes narrowed. "I can't believe you'd stoop so low."

"Sure you can."

Avra looked down at the carpet where she stabbed it with the heel of her lavender pump. "There's something you enjoy about giving me a hard time, isn't there?"

Appearing to contemplate her words, Sam tapped his fingers to the seductive curve of his mouth and smiled faintly.

Avra felt helpless to direct her gaze away from the gesture.

"I think you're right," he muttered.

"That's a first."

Any more that she might have said was silenced when his mouth crashed down on hers and he proceeded to kiss her hungrily. Resisting never occurred to Avra. She was determined to find out whether or not his build was credited to great tailoring or genetics.

Quickly she discovered it was all him. Heatedly she participated in the kiss, caressing his tongue over and under as she moaned unashamed.

Eventually it was Sam who pulled back, but only briefly. When he spied the wetness on her mouth, he couldn't resist another taste of her.

Faintly—*very* faintly—Avra realized she wasn't refusing him. She didn't want to refuse. Sam realized it, as well. Big hands cupping her delicate face, he drove his tongue deeper, craving more of her unique taste.

He ordered his need to cool and broke the kiss, stroking the tips of his thumbs across her moist, swollen lips. He waited until she brought her eyes to his. The smile he directed her way wasn't gloating, but tender. "I'm gonna have to work on changing your perception of me." He left her alone soon after.

Dazedly Avra stumbled back to her desk and leaned on one corner. It was some time before her breathing slowed.

Chapter 2

"Damn him." Avra blurted the words and shoved aside the file she'd been trying to review since she got up that morning.

Memories of the kiss with Sam Melendez that previous afternoon had her mind *and everything else* reacting to it. How dare he kiss her? How dare she want it? She despised the man, didn't she? They'd known each other for two years as business associates. Before that she'd known *of* him. He was the son of one of her father's oldest friends. From scores of female acquaintances she'd heard he was built, with looks to die for.

Once she'd officially met him, she realized those accolades were well deserved. But he shouldn't have kissed her. She shouldn't have wanted it and more still after he'd walked out of her office.

The fact that he wanted her in his bed was no secret.

He'd been up front about that from a few days after they'd first met to work on the Machine Melendez account with the *Ross Review*.

Avra cursed again. She had railed too long and too hard against strong, commanding men to give any part of herself to the likes of Sam Melendez. Strong, commanding, chauvinistic, politically incorrect men like Sam Melendez, she added. If he was simply one of her many male friends, she could find amusement in his lack of decorum and sexist nature. As it was directed toward her and he was ever so confident about taking her to bed, those less than admirable traits of his only grated more heavily on her nerves.

She stooped to the floor and began to collect the papers from the Wade Cornelius file that were scattered around the settee in her living room. She wondered if Sam knew how much of her hard-hearted approach was an act. It was unfortunately the only way she could ignore the way her body reacted to his presence and all the other things he did to get under her skin.

Sadly she'd devised no other method for resisting a reaction to his touch. If yesterday afternoon was any example, she was in serious trouble if he did that again.

Closing her eyes, she settled back against one of the settee's claw-footed legs and surrendered to a delicious shiver that raced through her body then. To no one else would she admit how very much she wanted him to kiss her again. When the phone rang her out of her daydream, Avra snapped to and decided *that* was the last thing she should be wanting.

Papers gathered though haphazardly arranged inside the manila envelope, Avra put the file on the settee and went to answer the phone. She laughed, noticing the name on the caller ID and cheerfully greeted her soon-to-be sister-in-law.

Setha Melendez sounded equally cheerful on the other end of the phone. That was to be expected, of course. Still, Avra felt the need to interrupt some of the cheer when Setha kept going on and on about the fun they were going to have when she came to stay at Sam's place.

"What the hell are you talking about?"

"Well, I… Well, it's all set for you to come and stay here for the shower party."

"Setha…who told you that?" Avra didn't need the answer. She already had it.

"Well, Sam said it was pretty much a done deal. Humph," Setha grunted, understanding the problem all too well. "Sorry."

"Don't worry about it. Just don't expect me out there."

"Uh-uh. No way, Av," the bride snapped. "I'm sorry Sam didn't tell you, but you can't back out now."

"Why the devil do you need *me* there?" Avra massaged the curls that tapered at her neck while pacing the short distance between the settee and the phone table. "You've got tons of friends—have one or all of 'em stay out there with you. Sam would love that." She grimaced over the thought.

"Don't bank on it," Setha muttered.

Avra stopped pacing. "Honey, what are you up to?'

"I'm hoping you can take Sam's mind off whatever's got him so edgy."

Avra had to laugh and it felt good to relieve a bit of the tension she struggled with that morning. "Honey, he's edgy over *me,* as usual."

"Avra, I honestly have no clue how he feels about you. I'm not so quick to say his feelings are bad, though."

There was another quick flash in Avra's mind about the kiss. The way he felt next to her—the way his mouth felt on hers, his tongue… She shook her head and quietly told herself to forget it.

"Besides, we can talk about the contract while you're here." Setha made the comment regarding the contract detailing the advertising renegotiations between the *Ross Review* and Machine Melendez airily enough but couldn't completely dismiss the urgency from her voice. "You can review it once more to be sure we're all on the same page with it all before the shooting for the ads starts in its entirety."

"Crap," Avra huffed, knocking a fist against the folds of the peach robe that draped past her ankles. "I don't have a problem with waiting, hashing out everything at the final meeting."

Setha huffed then, too. "Look, Avra…"

Avra felt her brow creasing. The tone of Setha's voice was fueled by more than the usual brother/sister agitations.

"There's something different—Sam's…always been protective, but this… It's more than normal."

"His baby sister's gettin' married, hon. That's a big deal," Avra softly pointed out.

"Yeah…I just hoped he'd loosen up with Carson Arroyo out of the picture. I've tried to get him to talk about whatever's goin' on but he just clams up. It's just him and me out here and I'm 'bout fed up with his mood."

"Right…" Avra rubbed the creases in her brow then,

understanding the woman's frustration. "Honey, um… you know you *are* a grown woman. You could always stay with Khouri. You guys *are* about to get married."

"I know it's stupid and old-fashioned." Setha's laughter came out brief across the phone line. "I just felt like it's the least I could do since I really did just spring all this on them. They didn't even know I was seeing anyone for Pete's sake."

Avra strolled back to sit on the arm of a chair near the phone table. "Did they give you a hard time about it?"

"Oh, no! Not even—which is a real surprise. They all like Khouri. They're happy for me but I think they're afraid they'll lose me once I become a wife."

"Well…they're not altogether wrong about that." Avra had settled into big-sister mode, always eager to offer an ear to listen.

"This is different, though." Setha's voice had gone softer. "I virtually closed myself off to them when I was investigating all that stuff about Carson Arroyo. Staying with Sam's the least I can do to make myself more available to them—for a little while longer anyway."

"So go stay with Mr. Dan." Avra referred to Setha's father and a sudden smile curved her mouth. "You'd get no argument from me about coming to stay over then."

"Sorry, girl, even big, bad Danilo Melendez wasn't willing to fight with Sam when he roared about me staying here with him."

Avra felt herself losing the battle.

"So? Will you come?"

Avra broke into a frustrated dance-jerk on the settee and rolled her eyes. "I'll be there." She managed to keep her voice level. Silently she acknowledged the part she'd played in riling Sam with talk of Carson Arroyo's motives. She couldn't help smiling over the sound of Setha giggling and yay-ing on the other end of the line.

"I'll be there today after work."

"Oh, thanks, Av. We're gonna have so much fun."

"Right. Fun."

"Oh…stop that and don't worry," Setha ordered and broke the connection seconds after.

The phone resumed its ring half a beat later. Avra laughed when she answered.

"Don't worry, I won't change my mind."

"I hope not," Sam said. "Aside from yes, *that* would be my second-favorite answer from you."

"Keep dreaming. What do you want?" She rolled her eyes, attempting to ward off her reaction to the sound of his deep laughter rumbling across the landline. "What is it, Sam?" she insisted.

"Just calling to see if you want me to send a car to the *Review* after work."

"Ah…" Avra stood from the settee. "Is this about Setha's shower? The particulars of which you didn't feel the need to share with me?"

Again, Sam chuckled. "Sorry 'bout that. Must've slipped my mind."

"Humph. I can see how easily that could happen."

Sam's laughter was a bit more resonant in response to her dig. "Anyway, the ranch is pretty far out. I figured you might be too worn-out to make the drive after a full day."

"Gee, Sam, I must say you continue to amaze me. I wouldn't have thought you capable enough to come up with such a thoughtful plan."

"I told you yesterday that I'm working to change your opinion of me."

She'd been doing such a fine job of maintaining her stony demeanor, Avra thought. She coughed in reply to his mention of his office visit and a flashback to the kiss filled her mind for the second time that morning.

"I'll be fine, Sam. I'll drive my own car."

"Mmm…in case you need to make an escape."

"Something like that."

"I would never force you, Av," he said once silence held the line for a lengthy span.

She refused to ask whether he was referring to the ride he'd offered.

"So I guess that means you won't force me on this trip to Kemah, right?"

"I'm not totally rehabilitated yet." Laughter carried on his gravelly, deep words. "You can't expect me to get rid of all my bad habits just like that."

"Well, then here's your chance to make progress."

"I'm very stubborn, too." He made a tsking sound over the phone. "Another bad habit to work on. Sorry, Av."

"Such a jackass," she hissed below her breath. "I'll get my own ride." She slammed the phone down on his laughter.

Not surprising, the ringing resumed again.

"Damn you," she greeted.

Khouri burst into laughter then. "Hell, girl, I swear it's too early in the morning even for *me* to be on your bad side."

"Sorry, Khou…" she groaned, knocking a fist to her forehead when she heard her brother's voice. "Just had a bad call."

"So Dad got to you, too, huh?"

"No…what's up?"

"I was calling to ask if you knew what this meeting was for."

"Meeting? Today?"

"Ten a.m. sharp."

"Damn." The wall clock above her fireplace read 9:10 a.m. "Well…maybe it's somethin' good," she hurriedly reasoned while collecting files and shoving them into her white leather valise. "How'd he sound when he called you?"

"Pissed. I'm guessing this ain't one of those pats-on-the-back meetings."

Avra stilled, thinking back to the tense conversation with her father the day before. "Guess we'll find out soon," she said, deciding against sharing the father-daughter discussion with her brother.

"See you there, all right?"

"Yeah." She waited for Khouri to break the connection first. "Damn," she muttered.

"Thanks for comin out, B. I know it was short notice." Sam was shaking hands with Chief of Detectives Bradley Crest when the man arrived in his office at Machine Melendez.

"Not a problem." Brad clapped Sam's shoulder when they were done shaking hands. "I've been meaning to come out or call to check on Mr. Dan. He didn't look too good when I left that day." Brad's blue eyes harbored a probing intensity as he removed his hat.

"It's not easy for him to hear these murders are targeting his employees." Sam tapped his index knuckle against the corner of his mouth as he thought of his father. "Man's not as young as he used to be." Something about the muttered acknowledgment struck a chord with Sam. Tugging on the cuffs of the shirt hanging outside his trousers, he went over to lean against his desk.

"Everything all right, Sam?" Brad worried the brim of his hat.

"Any new developments in this thing, Brad? Specifically, have y'all found any connections between Martino Viejo and the other victims?"

Brad bowed his head. He knew what Sam was really asking. "So far no links between Viejo and the address the others shared."

Samson didn't mind letting his relief show. He drew both hands through his dark straight hair and let out a sigh.

"The guy—Viejo—sure accomplished a lot in a short span of time."

"Yeah," Sam murmured with a grunt meant to be a laugh. "And I hadn't even heard of him till he died."

"From what we've gathered so far, he kept a pretty low profile but made a respected name for himself dealing with the public on behalf of MM."

"Guess that explains why dad's so upset over his death."

"Makes sense." Brad settled his lean, wiry frame into a chair. "Losin' an employee that valuable…gotta hurt."

Sam understood Brad's point. For some reason he just didn't buy it. He chose to keep that part of his opinion to himself.

"You still don't have a lead into who killed him?" Sam asked instead.

It was Brad's turn to grunt a humorless laugh. "All we know is who *didn't* kill him. Whoever it was cleaned up very well behind himself."

"Can you pin the other murders on Arroyo?"

Brad looked uneasy then. "None of this goes past this room." His stony expression brooked no argument.

Sam only spread his hands, silently implying that he knew that better than anyone.

"Hell—" Brad threw up a wave "—this thing's got me edgier than a deer in headlights. Whole thing's a mess." He pushed out of the chair he'd occupied and stalked the spacious scope of Sam's office. "The leads we *think* we have all tend to crisscross and fizzle. We got absolutely nothin' to go on 'cept an address no map or GPS can locate."

Sam was back to massaging his jaw as he considered all the detective shared.

"Truth is—" Brad sighed "—we can only pin two of the murders on Arroyo—*he* was sloppy. Aside from the evidence we recovered, those murders pointed to him because they were so similar. The others…" Brad studied the stitching in the brim of the hat. "Once you toss in the similarities with the vics, nothin' else seemed to fit."

Sam frowned. "What the hell does that mean?"

"That either Arroyo switched up his style from sloppy to smart for three of the murders or there's a second killer."

The silence that settled then was only interrupted by the shrill ring of Brad's cell. Less than a minute later, he was making his way out of the office.

Sam remained seated on the corner of his desk, deep in thought.

* * *

"Surprised to see you here, man," Luc Anton greeted once he'd knocked on Danilo's office door and strolled inside.

Dan shrugged, barely looking up from the papers he shuffled. "Important for the staff to be reassured given what's happened." He stopped with the papers and clenched his fists. "Tino's death… It's a huge loss."

"And I commend your courage for being here," Luc noted; his voice was soft yet the subtle hint of curiosity was there.

Dan heard it and smiled as he returned to sit behind his desk. "Say what you came to say."

"What? I'm commending—"

"Luc."

"Tino's death could open up a can of worms wide enough to swallow us."

"Martino Viejo was a good worker."

Luc's brow creased, adding more wrinkles to his weather-beaten skin. "And you think that means he didn't keep certain reminders of earlier times? Let's not forget that was how he rose so high."

"He would've never resorted to blackmail," Dan snapped.

"Are you serious? Or are you getting Martino Viejo confused with the staff or your sons who think the sun rises and sets with you?" Luc spat a soft, vicious curse. "You're a fool if you think the cops won't find something while investigating that kid's murder—something that could put us all in trouble." He raised a finger. "You need to get in front of this before it's too late."

Dan's pitch stare narrowed. "That a threat, Lucas?"

"It's a fact, old friend." With those words, Luc left the room.

"He called in *all* the reporters?" Avra was asking Khouri when they stepped into the main meeting room at *Ross Review.*

The area was filled to capacity with writers, editors and anyone else even remotely involved with the department. Khouri and Avra found two seats close together but not in the same row. There were hushed, indecipherable conversations. Someone complained about there not being more coffee at the buffet that had been set up along a far wall. Shortly afterward a door slammed and all heads turned to Basil Ross, who had just entered.

Avra turned in her seat to look at Khouri, who simply grimaced and shook his head. They both knew the look their father wore. Basil Ross was not a happy man.

"I'll make this quick," Basil said just after claiming his spot standing behind the long table at the front of the room.

"All research and reporting on the MM murders is to stop at once."

Conversation filled the room once again in a barreling wave. Questions flew from all corners and at varying decibels.

"Why?"

"Why now?"

"We got so much uncovered, sir!"

"Working on the MM story now constitutes a firing offence."

Basil's announcement fueled more conversation but at a much softer volume.

"Questions?" he asked, eyeing the crowd speculatively.

No raised hands emerged.

"Very well."

Conversation returned to its deafening volume once Basil exited the room. Everyone was on their feet, except for Avra.

Chapter 3

Avra checked her wristwatch. James Purdy was always ready and waiting with her car door open and engine idling when she called down to let him know she was on her way out. Unless the man was sick, which didn't happen often, he was at his post.

That day, however, her car door wasn't open and the engine wasn't idling. In fact, the Lexus coupe wasn't there at all. James Purdy stood just outside the entrance to the parking staff office. He appeared to be in fine health and spirits as he talked, laughed and shared a bag of potato chips with Sam Melendez. When James caught sight of Avra, though, he straightened from his leaning stance along the brick wall leading into the parking deck.

"Afternoon, Miss A." James tipped the brim of his navy blue cap.

"James." She cast a pointed look across her shoulder. "This is a first. Should I pick my car up some-place else?"

"Oh, uh…" Uncertainty crept into the man's kind dark eyes as though he were slowly realizing some-thing was amiss. "Well, Mr. M…." He glanced back at Samson. "He said you wouldn't be needing it tonight."

"Oh, did he?" The expression Avra turned on Sam was nowhere near as polite as the one she'd given James.

Sam brushed crumbs from his hands while bracing off the wall. "Thanks for the chips, Jay." He pressed the nearly empty bag to James's chest as he walked past to take Avra's upper arm.

"Ah, ah, ah…" he urged when she stiffened in re-sponse to his thumb brushing the bare flesh beneath the cap sleeve of her blouse. "Don't make a scene now."

"What do you think you're doing?" Avra's voice was as tight as the phony smile she wore for James's benefit while Sam escorted her from the parking deck to the smaller lot, which sat catty-corner from the *Review*'s main entrance.

He gave her a slight tug when she tried to quicken her steps. "I'm taking you to my sister's party."

"Told you I have my own ride."

"And *I* told *you* that I'm tryin' to turn over a new leaf." He gave her a wink when she glared at him. "Leavin' a *little* thing like you to make your way out to my ranch all by your lonesome just didn't seem like the gentlemanly thing to do."

"Only you could make the *gentlemanly* thing to do sound self-serving and suspicious." Her voice was still tight as their steps carried them into the lot.

Sam pressed a hand to the center of his broad chest and turned her to him when they approached his truck.

"Will you ever think better of me, Avra Ross?"

"Highly unlikely."

Soon after voicing the statement, Avra felt the unyielding metal of the passenger-side door behind her back. Crowded against the truck and Samson's equally unyielding frame, she was kissed—and thoroughly. Soft moans gathered instantly at the back of her throat and Avra didn't care how loudly they sounded. She moved to her toes, positioning herself more comfortably against him, and thrust her tongue hungrily against his.

Sam had released his hold on her arms the second he crushed her mouth beneath his. He kept his hands sprawled on either side of her along the door of the F-150. Somehow, and he couldn't fathom a guess as to how, he managed not to touch her except to kiss her.

Avra tunneled her hands into his hair, shivering as the soft mass brushed her fingers. She scraped her nails along the onyx whiskers that darkened his copper-toned face and toyed with the buttons along the short-sleeved shirt hanging outside his dark denims. When he at last showed mercy and broke the kiss in midstroke of his tongue, she let her head fall to his shoulder. Desperately she worked to slow her breathing and shivered anew when he nuzzled his nose against her ear.

"Guess I'll have to keep trying, huh?" He looked down into her face, frowning slightly as he studied her ever more intently.

Avra could only press her lips together in response to his query. Sam appeared satisfied and eventually stepped back to open the passenger door and wave her inside.

* * *

"What are you doing?" she asked when they arrived at her building and he shut down the truck's smooth engine.

"I'm going in."

"Why?"

"Are you packed?"

"Yes, and I only have to grab my bag and I'll be right out."

A smile tugged the shamefully sensual curve of his wide mouth. "You're lying," he said after studying her for a beat.

Avra rolled her eyes past the windshield. "So what'd you ask me for, then?"

"To see what kind of lie you'd come up with."

Avra opened the door and left the truck cab in a huff. Sam chuckled and left the vehicle with ease.

Of course the guards knew Sam. Almost everyone in Houston worked for or knew someone who worked for Machine Melendez.

"Evenin', Miss Avra," Claude Bevins greeted and tipped his cap before grinning broadly at Sam and extending his hand for a shake.

"Need us to have your truck parked, man?" Joel Henries asked after he'd shaken hands with Sam, as well.

Grinning, Sam waited for Avra's coffee-brown eyes to come to his dark ones. "Thanks, guys, but we won't be long. Ms. Ross is spending the night at my place."

The look she sent his way should have reduced Sam to a pool of waste on the lobby floor. It had had a similar effect on others. Sam's grin merely broadened when she left him standing with the guards.

"Better head on up before she changes her mind, boys." He clapped Joel's shoulder and slanted a wink toward Claude and sprinted off.

Avra didn't bother holding open the elevator door. She was only intent on closing out the sound of Sam's laughter with the guards. The cherrywood doors were almost sealed when a hand slid between them. Sam eased inside the car a few seconds later. Avra slapped him as soon as the doors closed at his back.

"High school was never my favorite game to play, Sam."

"What?" He raised both hands in an innocent move that mocked the grin on his face. He sidestepped her in the small confines of the car, when she moved to hit him again.

"You *are* spending the night at my place, right?"

"Oh, please."

"What?"

"You jackass, you know that's not what you wanted them to think."

Taking the risk of being hit again, Sam stepped close. "What is it you think I wanted them to think? Ahh…" Enviously long lashes shielded his eyes then. "That you're going to my place to have sex with me…"

Avra snorted. "That'll never happen."

"Is that right?" He slammed a fist against the elevator's stop button without looking toward the control panel. "Never?" he probed.

There wasn't much space to retreat. Correction: there was *no* space to retreat when one shared an elevator with the likes of Samson Melendez. Avra cleared her throat but refused to show any other trace of unease.

"Is this *crowding* supposed to intimidate me or have

me panting like an idiot and hoping you'll do something I didn't know I wanted?"

The unexpected challenging inquiry softened Sam's copper-kissed features with thoughtfulness instead of humor.

"Have you put much consideration into me doing something like that, Av?"

She rolled her eyes, edging away from him in one cool move. "Is this your way of making me change my opinion of you?"

Sam leaned on the opposite wall of the car and raked his pitch stare down the rigid line of her back, which she'd turned his way. "What's the point in tryin' to better myself when you've already told me it's pointless?" He studied the lines in his palms and waited for her answer.

Avra looked up at the floor number, which had lit up when Sam stopped the car. "I'd never tell you it's pointless to better yourself, Sam." She turned her head a fraction. "It's only pointless to think bettering yourself will get me in your bed." She didn't need to turn around. She could feel his wide frame less than an inch away.

"I never said it had to be *my* bed."

His words preceded touch. Avra bit her upper lip and swallowed when one of his big hands smothered a small yet full breast. Not long after, he'd worked the nipple into a firm nub beneath her shirt and eased it past the barrier of her bra.

Avra didn't try resisting. She already knew she couldn't. Instead she moved against the subtle, pleasurable massage. Barely there, breathy sounds slipped past her mouth as she pressed her nipple deeper into his palm. She was moments from turning to him when she snapped to.

Sam had hit the elevator's stop button again. The car continued its ascent. He put space between them, giving Avra time to fix her clothes and collect herself. She kept her back turned for the duration of the trip. Once the doors whispered open, she bolted from the car.

Alone then, Sam allowed his smug playfulness to vanish. Pressing a thumb to the corner of his eye, he sighed heavily. "Nice, Sam, nice..." he muttered.

He left the car reluctantly and was more than a little surprised to find Avra holding open the door when he arrived at the condo. He crossed the threshold as reluctantly as he'd left the elevator. His dark gaze was astute, alert as he observed his surroundings in the event that an anvil or some other destructive device might come crashing down on his head. He moved no farther than the foyer.

"Drink?" Avra slammed the door and moved past him and into the condominium.

Sam continued to tread slowly. Hands in his pockets, the alertness in his eyes transitioned into something more akin to curiosity. He watched her kick off the chocolate pumps that complemented the mocha and tan of her blouse and accentuated her shapely long legs beneath the flaring hem of her wrap skirt.

Avra prepared a gin tonic, took a sip then wiggled her glass in silent inquiry to Sam.

"Got any Jack?" he asked, relaxing just a smidge.

She dutifully prepared the drink and then crossed the room while sipping her gin. She handed him a beaded glass and waited for him to drink.

"Why is my dad protecting yours?" she asked when he nodded his approval of the liquor.

Samson blinked deliberately, his attempt at ease sailing right into oblivion. "What the hell are you talkin' about?"

"Right." Avra shook her head. "I see your dad shares about as much as mine does." She demurely sipped more of her drink.

Sam downed the rest of the Jack Daniel's. "I'm still confused, Av."

"My dad called a meeting today and basically threatened to fire his reporters if they so much as sniffed at the Melendez story. Why would he do that? Protect MM that way?"

Sam was twirling the empty beaded glass in his hands. "I haven't got one damn clue, Av."

"Would you tell me if you did?"

"Darlin'—" he grinned wearily "—I sure as hell would if I knew where to start. All I have are bits and pieces of junk that may or may not be anything."

Avra believed him. Especially since her own luck at finding answers had proven to be just as dismal. She was certainly in no position to share what she had, either.

"I'll get my stuff packed," she said and set her glass on an end table before scooping up the shoes she'd kicked off. "Won't be long," she called over her shoulder.

Alone in the living room, Sam went to help himself to another drink. He scanned the room and looked thoughtfully toward the mound of files and papers lying on the coffee table.

* * *

"What the hell is this?" Brad Crest's tanned face was a study in frustration and confusion. One of his men had just set the last of eight boxes on the counter in his office at the precinct.

"Boxes contain things taken from Martino Viejo's home," Detective Gregory Roth explained.

Brad straightened on the sofa at the mention of the latest Machine Melendez murder victim. "What do you mean *things?*"

Greg shrugged, his low brow crinkling with agitation. "Just that—a bunch of stuff that could mean nothin', but given the fact that we're leavin' no stone unturned *and* the nature of some of this stuff…"

Brad braced his elbows to his knees, his mouth curved downward as he considered Greg's point. "Show me what you got." He shrugged.

Greg motioned to the other man in the room, and together they brought four of the boxes to the coffee table set before the long sofa in Brad's office. Dutifully, Greg passed his boss a box of latex gloves and waited on Brad to put them in place.

Mild surprise mixed with curiosity soon claimed Brad's face. Despite the latex gloves, he seemed hesitant about touching the photo he stared down at. "Is that…?"

Greg was already nodding. "Senator Herbert Willins."

Carefully, Brad picked up the plastic-sleeved photograph. Willins and Martino Viejo were both grinning broadly, arms linked about one another's shoulders. A luxury yacht had been captured in the background of the picture.

"I knew this guy's job put him in the company of some pretty influential folks, but…" Brad's voice trailed off into silence as he studied other photos of Martino Viejo looking chummy with other influential types.

"Dawson's son?" Brad took a closer look at the picture of Viejo and the lieutenant governor's oldest son.

Greg tugged on his earlobe. "The man himself's in a few, as well," he said in reference to Lieutenant Governor Logan Dawson.

Brad whistled. "Impressive list." He tossed the photo back to the coffee table. "Makes it even more pressin' for us to find out who's behind this ASAP."

"We're just now finishing up documenting all the photos," Greg explained, grimacing toward the evidence boxes. "They'll be on the way to the lab soon, but there's more here than snapshots, boss. With your permission, I'd like to request extra help to go through it all."

"Well, what else have you found?"

"Boxes of journals from his garage." Greg scratched at the thinning hair at the crown of his head. "A lot of water-rotted crap. It'll be a tedious task pullin' anything off those pages—may take a while."

"I understand. All right, then, pick your people and I'll sign off on it." Brad leaned back on the sofa, his eyes narrowed toward his second in command. "Somethin' else on your mind, Captain?"

Greg gave a jerky nod to the other detective in the room. "Bring Floyd and Cooper in here," he instructed and then went to sit in the chair opposite Brad. "Boxes on the counter are filled with CDs and dictated cassette tapes. We haven't listened in and they still need to be dusted, but given the circles this guy runs in, there may be stuff that needs to be handled delicately…"

"And?" Brad nodded when Greg watched him expectantly.

"Well, sir, I, um. Maybe you'd want to handle it yourself, given…"

"Given my friendship with the Melendez family." Brad grimaced.

"Sir, this thing already stinks to high heaven." Greg leaned forward, mimicking Brad, who sat with his elbows on his knees. "Who knows what we'll find in that stuff?" He gave another jerky nod to the counter.

"Thank you for caring, son." Brad fixed Greg with an earnest look. "Friendships are the last things I'm tryin' to preserve just now. Grab anybody you can spare from other cases and put 'em on this, all right?"

Greg nodded once and stood. "I'll send someone in for this stuff."

Alone in the office, Brad flexed his hands still encased in the latex. He tilted his head at an odd angle when he noticed Martino Viejo in pictures with Dan Melendez and board chairman Lucas Anton.

Turning his gaze toward the boxes on the counter, Brad groaned and fell back against the sofa.

Avra waited quietly, watching Sam at the coffee table browsing her file on Wade Cornelius. "See anything interesting?" she asked when he looked her way.

"You've been busy," he commended.

Avra set down the bag she'd packed. "Aren't you the one always telling me I have no life except for being a slave driver to my staff and giving you a hard time?" She tugged at the long, lightweight scarf around her neck and shrugged. "Guess that leaves me lots of time for conducting homegrown investigations into unsolved crimes."

"But Wade Cornelius died of natural causes."

"Did he, now?"

"These papers tell you otherwise?" Sam shook some of the pages in question.

"Don't know." Avra batted the fringes of the scarf back and forth against her palms. "So far they've only served to give me a massive headache. Wade's notes were all over the place."

"Yeah." Sam's sleek brows drew close in mild criticism as he scanned the journalist's haphazard method of note taking. "Probably a writer's thing," he reasoned.

"Humph." Avra eased her hands into the back pockets of her jeans. "Maybe that's why I was always so bad at it."

Grinning easily, Sam's gaze slid back to the page he held. His eyes narrowed, and after a moment, he tilted his head and drew the sheet closer.

"You find something?" Avra pulled her hands from her pockets and moved to the sofa in order to peer across his shoulder.

"Do you know what this is?" Sam was brushing his index finger across a number.

"Uh-uh, but I've come across it more than once in his notes." She sat on the back of the sofa. "I feel like I should know what it is, though."

Sam nodded while massaging his jaw. "Me, too," he said.

Chapter 4

Samson wore a frown when he walked into the kitchen bright and early the next morning.

Setha looked up from sweetening her coffee to fix her brother with a dazzling smile that matched the sparkle in her eyes. "Well, my, my, I didn't think you got up before noon on Saturdays."

"Where is she?" Sam grunted.

Setha's beaming smile brightened, if that were possible. "Don't worry. She's sleeping like a baby. I think this place calms her—almost like she belongs here." Setha practically sang the words.

Sam groaned. "Please don't start with that stuff, Set."

"What?" Setha's voice raised an octave higher. "I'm just stating the obvious."

"Right." Sam's frown darkened.

"Oh, please." She waved him off and sprinted to

the refrigerator for cream. "I dare you to deny that her being here is why you rushed—"

"I never rush."

"All right—" Setha waved her hands in an accommodating fashion "—*arrived* downstairs on a Saturday way earlier than usual."

"Goin' for a ride." Sam's mumbled words were almost inaudible.

"Want some company?" Setha hooked a thumb in a belt loop on her denim cutoffs.

Sam rolled his eyes and went to look for the key to the barn that housed his prized stallions. "Not if *this* is all you're gonna talk about."

"Nope, you've told me all I need to know." She sipped her coffee happily.

Again, Sam rolled his eyes and left the kitchen without another word. Setha downed another hearty gulp of her coffee and ran after her brother.

Avra had awakened a half an hour earlier. Instead of heading down to the kitchen, she took up residence at the calico-cushioned window seat. There she enjoyed the rear view of the S. Melendez Ranch. It was a magnificent spread.

As magnificent as the owner?

"Stop," she ordered with a shake of her head and an angry rub across the bridge of her nose. She glanced toward the night table to read the clock that said 8:35 a.m.

"Go back to sleep." She tugged the peach terry robe about her slender form but made no move to leave the seat. "Lord knows the bed was a dream," she said amid a yawn.

In spite of that, Avra feared she'd only roll around in

it wide-awake. Thankfully sleep had visited her quickly and deeply the night before. She'd awakened refreshed, but her mind raced the second she opened her eyes and realized where she was. Knowing Samson Melendez slept under the same roof was disconcerting at best. He wanted her, and all she had to do was reach out and accept the pleasure he offered...

Avra shook her head again and added a groan. She tried to focus on the beauty beyond the second-story window and saw Sam and his sister walking toward one of the many large barns in the distance. A voice taunted Avra then, telling her that sleeping with Samson Melendez didn't mean she had to confess eternal love and devotion to him.

Sleeping with him could be so...mmm... Avra drew her knees up to her chin and took delight in the faint tingle stirred by the thought. A thin slice of reality nudged its way in amid the sweeter thoughts. It was most effective in smothering the pleasurable feeling she enjoyed.

Sleeping with Sam Melendez wouldn't be a decision she could make, follow through on and walk away from. A man like that demanded much, took more, demanded more still and then left a woman breathless and willing to give—or take—whatever else he craved.

She'd seen too many women fall victim to such nonsense. She'd promised herself such idiocy was not for her. Pleasure was always acceptable but not all the drama and heartache that tended to crop up. That, in addition to the tendency women had for losing themselves when the frothy delight of a new relationship turned into a maelstrom once that relationship soured.

She never allowed things to go that far with a man.

She ended it all before that even became a possibility. She knew ending it all wouldn't be so easy with Sam Melendez. Easy? It'd be downright difficult as hell.

What's more, Avra knew…with everything in her, she knew Sam had the power to turn her wild, mindless, oblivious to all except the pleasure his single touch provided. He'd have her panting and eager to do anything he desired. Would she care?

She doubted she'd care at all.

Setha Melendez's bridal shower was the stuff of princesses. Samson had spared no expense or effort to make the gathering as special as possible for his sister. As a result every woman in attendance felt as special as the bride-to-be.

No one would have guessed the house and property closest to it rested on a ranch. Flowers of varying colors and variety flooded almost every corner of the lower area. Already one of Texas's most plush homes, the main house at S. Melendez Ranch garnered many more accolades that day.

Despite the decor and tribute to all things lovely, Avra wasn't overwhelmed. Bridal showers and other such "girly" rites of passage had never been her cup of tea. Not until she realized how bowled over Raquel and Fiona were by them did she understand the true value of little sisters. When Rocky and Fee arrived to join the rest of Setha's excited friends, Avra gracefully made her escape with a glass of her favorite wine.

The evening was surprisingly cool, perfect for a stroll around the gorgeous grounds in the strapless, pale peach frock she wore with matching open-toed sandals. Using the time alone, Avra revisited her thoughts from earlier that day. She asked herself whether she had the nerve to walk right up to Samson Melendez and tell him what she wanted and what she'd never settle for.

A moment later she was stopping dead in her tracks.

"Dammit," she muttered, the sudden stop causing a bit of the sauvignon blanc to slosh up past the sides of her goblet. She could see Sam through a wide bay window of what looked to be a den on the lower level of his home. He appeared to be deep in concentration.

Avra moved closer down the walkway leading to the window. There she studied the man for a time, unconscious of the fact that she was lightly nibbling the mouth of her wineglass, while her eyes trailed him in blatant wantonness.

As if he'd sensed an intrusion on his solitude, Sam turned his head and looked right at her.

At least Avra *thought* he was looking her way. Surely he couldn't see her in the dark through a window from a lit room? she thought. She was wrong. Rooted to her spot, she watched him cross the room and open a door she hadn't noticed before.

"You comin' in or just gonna stand out there invading my privacy?"

Flexing her fingers about the stem of the glass, Avra moved forward as though there were nothing out of the ordinary about her standing outside in the dark. "I wasn't invading your privacy. You were only... What *are* you doing?" she asked, once inside the den.

Sam smirked, shaking his head in spite of himself. "I come in here to unwind."

Accepting the response, she nodded and curved her mouth downward to appear impressed by the surroundings. "I can see why." She complimented the room.

Sam's smirk merged into a more content smile. He seemed truly pleased by her words.

"This is nice." Avra didn't want to lose herself in his gaze or his words so she complimented the mural that took up one full wall of the den.

The compliment was no idle stab at conversation. She was amazed by the detail of the piece. It drew her in, so much so that she was reaching out to touch the wall. She quickly drew back her hand.

"Go ahead," Sam permitted, not realizing how captivated he was by the sight of her in his home and appreciating something that meant so much to him.

"This is incredible." Lightly she trailed her fingers across the bumpy stucco texture of the wall to outline the images captured in the work. "Who did this?"

"Friend from college." Sam eased his hands into side pockets of his brown cargo pants. "He's an animator out in California."

"It's exquisite." Her eyes were still riveted on the work. "I'd love to meet him. Do you know how to contact him?"

Sam smothered a groan, having lost interest in the discussion. He didn't try to deny that he was agitated as much by Avra's interest in his artist friend as he was by the fact that he was agitated at all.

"He didn't draw the thing from inspiration, Av," Sam said, his voice a bit edgy when she turned for a response to her question. "He was working from a photo."

"Nice." Avra didn't acknowledge Sam's attitude but went back to admiring the stunning mural. "Sam?" She moved closer to the wall and frowned. "Is that your dad?"

The question buffed away the rough edges of his mood and he smiled a bit. "It is."

"Who took the picture?" Avra turned to Sam when he once again hesitated with his answer.

Finally he shrugged. "Your dad."

"Dammit," Fiona Ross snapped.

"Hey, hey! That word is *not* to be used during my one and *only* shower!"

"Where've *you* been, Seth? A woman saying *dammit* don't always mean somethin' bad!"

Everyone broke into waves of laughter.

Setha frowned, though, when she saw Fiona standing.

"I'm on call." Fiona spread her hands and grimaced apologetically. "I tried to get out of it."

"It's okay, girl. You're savin' lives," Setha said, rounding the table to pull the woman into a hug.

"Well, I'll make it up to you anyway. Hey, I know." Her slanting stare sparkled when she pulled back from embracing Setha. "You could marry my brother. Women say he's quite hot."

The laughter positively thundered then. Setha and Fiona shared another tight hug. Then, Fiona called out her good-nights to the other guests and hurried off the patio.

"Where the hell did Av go?" Raquel was asking then.

"Humph." Setha smoothed down the folds of her flaring mauve wrap skirt before she settled onto a lounge chair. "If my talent for reading people is right on, and I know it is, Avra hates these kinds of parties."

"Ha!" Raquel confirmed the suspicion about her big sister.

"Mmm-hmm, and Sam's been tryin' to get a minute alone with her since she got here… Hopefully they're off someplace together," Setha shared.

"But isn't it World War II every time they're in the same room?" Raquel cautioned.

"Yeah…" Only a hint of Setha's smugness vanished. "I forgot about that part." She waved to a passing server. "Could I get another drink over here?"

Moments later the women were dissolving into more laughter.

"It's quiet," Sam noted as he and Avra strolled the hallway. "Sounds like you missed the party."

"Just as well." She drew a hand through the riot of short, glossy curls tumbling over her head. "They really aren't my thing."

Sam kept both hands in his pockets as he walked. "That go for bridal parties or just parties in general?"

"Oh, I love a good party."

Sam chuckled at her quick reply. "So it's just the bridal ones, huh?"

"Yep…just the bridal ones. Those I can definitely do without."

"Any particular reason?" Sam bowed his head when he asked the question.

"Never enough men there." Avra joined in with Sam when he laughed more fully.

They had reached her room at the end of the second-floor corridor. Avra was still under the effects of her earlier burst of laughter and was still chuckling softly when Sam put his hand over the knob to keep her from opening the door.

"Could you be serious and tell me the real reason?"

Avra blinked, studying the bottomless pools of his very black gaze. "About the party? That *is* the real reason."

"And not a fear of commitment?" he challenged.

She leaned back against the door. "What do you need my opinion on that for? I'd say you know all there is to know there."

He leaned against the opposite side of the door. "I don't have that fear." He kept his hand over the knob.

"Oh. right. It's *your* turn to be honest now, Sam." Avra rolled her eyes amusedly. "Let us not forget your numerous social interests." Her eyes lowered when he moved in to easily crowd her between the door and his big frame.

"I may not have a fear of commitment but I sure as hell am afraid of making a mistake."

"Good." Avra swallowed, blinking slowly as she tried to anticipate his next move.

Sam moved his hand from the doorknob and brought it to her chin. "That's *very* good," he murmured a split second before his lips were sealed to hers.

Avra was moaning before his tongue began to mate with hers. Once they were in the midst of a full-blown kiss, she buried her fingers in his thick hair, arching herself against his chest and crying out against the delicious friction the move stirred. She could have slid right down the length of the door; she was melting just that quickly.

Sam prevented that by propping one thigh between both of hers once he'd used his free hand to tug the hem of her dress. Afterward he took full advantage, moving his hand from her chin and slipping both of them beneath her dress. One hand squeezed an ample buttock while the other flexed about her thigh, allowing the hand on her bottom more room to roam.

Avra let her head fall back to the door. The move left her neck bare and beckoning his lips, which stroked and nibbled the coffee-brown column. His long, wide fingers were skirting the hem of her panties but they didn't delve past the crotch of the undergarment. Instead his thumb began a provocative assault on her sex. Avra bit her lip, moving naughtily and without shame in response to the orgasm-inducing massage. When he pulled his hands from beneath her dress, she used her fist to thump the brick wall of his chest.

Sam wanted to see her and made quick work of tugging down the square bodice of the strapless frock. He filled his palms with her plump breasts and worshipped their image while applying a sensual thumb massage to the gradually puckering nipples. A faint obscenity lilted from his tongue and he replaced his thumb with his mouth.

Hungry suckling commenced and the expert finesse of it had Avra straining against the door as her hips writhed. Her nails raked his scalp as he intermittently feasted on one nipple and then the other.

In the back of her mind she recalled that the guests from the evening's party were bunking along that very hall. Given the volume of her moans, she could wake one or all of them easily. Besides, she couldn't do this. They couldn't do this, at least not there—not yet. Could they?

She squeezed her eyes shut and dug reluctantly for

the power to resist more of what he was giving to her. Just a little more, a quiet voice urged her. Just a little more and then back away... But she wouldn't back away. Avra knew that with utmost certainty. She'd craved the man for too long—that alone unsettled her enough to give her pause.

"Sam..." Her hands half curled into fists on his chest.

He responded by filling her mouth with his tongue, enticing hers to rotate, seek, withdraw and then re-engage. Sensation rumbled through her body like a raging wave and she obliged in kissing him back with equal fire. She pulled her mouth from his and rested her forehead to his collarbone.

"Sam, I can't..."

"At all or just with me?" His hand flexed on her hip as he fought to accept what she was telling him.

"Sam...we need to stop."

"I don't," he countered, hand twisting on the knob as he moved forward to back her inside the room.

She braced against his frame. She shook her head and regretted the agitation she could see pooling in his ebony stare.

He blinked, taking stock of his actions. "Right." Easing back, he let his hands fall from her body. He made a fist, pressing it to the wall as he bowed his head and deeply inhaled.

"Don't get comfortable in here," he was saying a few short moments later and looking pointedly past the doorway into the room. "We leave for Kemah to-morrow."

Avra steeled herself beneath the look he gave her. She could virtually feel the chill from the deep-set orbs.

When he moved down the hall, she told herself things were back to normal.

He despised her again.

Chapter 5

"Well, there she is!" Setha greeted when Avra arrived in the kitchen the next morning.

"Hey, hon." Avra spoke through a yawn and went over to hug Setha. "Sorry for walkin' out on the party."

"'S'okay. Me and Rocky had a great time with everybody. You were missed but we managed."

"What about Fee?" Avra inquired of her youngest sister while preparing a mug of breakfast tea.

"On call." Setha was already sipping coffee. "She had to leave early."

"Life of a doctor." Avra breathed, "It's why the girl has no life." She steeped a tea bag while reaching for the sugar bowl.

"She hated to go, but we were fine."

"Sorry I left." Avra sweetened her tea and hoped she sounded sincere.

"Well, I'm sure you were having more fun with Sam anyway."

Avra's spoon hit the counter with a clatter. She spun 180 degrees. "What?"

"Don't even deny you were with Sam."

"Don't you have wedding stuff to tend to?" Avra grabbed her tea and brought it to the wood-paneled kitchen island.

Setha laughed.

"No, seriously—don't y'all have to pick out china or somethin'?"

"Well, speak of the devil." Setha's dark eyes sparkled even more brilliantly when her fiancé walked into the sunny kitchen.

"What's up, Av?" Khouri greeted his sister on the way to pulling Setha up high against his chest. Shamelessly she wrapped her legs around his back and met his kiss with an eager fire.

"Could y'all please take that stuff upstairs." Avra only pretended to be agitated. In actuality she was smiling at the love and happiness surrounding the couple. Giving the betrothed a measure of privacy, she went to drop a slice of bread in the six-slotted toaster.

Khouri and Setha slid out of their embrace just as Sam walked into the kitchen through the back door. Avra looked up and caught the barely there glance he threw her way before he greeted Khouri.

"Want some breakfast, babe?" Setha asked, already moving to slip off the tall chair at the island and see to her fiancé's needs.

"Thanks, but no." He dropped a lingering kiss to the corner of her mouth. "We should get this business out of the way so I can have the rest of the day with you."

The stern expression Sam was wearing when he walked in from securing his horse in the stable began to soften. He couldn't help seeing the devotion between his sister and her husband-to-be. He shook off the syrupy emotions before they could work any real magic on his sour mood.

"What business?" he asked when the couple drew apart.

Khouri opened the leather satchel he'd brought along with him. "Contract's ready for you and Av to sign." He withdrew the document from a clear portfolio. "Then me and Seth can officially wash our hands of this." He pushed the paper across the counter space.

Sam nodded, eyes following the path of his fingers as they trailed the words on the page in a brief scan. "Thanks to both of you." He looked up to nod at Khouri and then Setha. "I know it took a lot to get this done, but it's appreciated. We couldn't seem to do a damn thing right."

As one of the "we" Sam referred to, Avra bristled and turned to remove the lone slice of toast that had just popped up crisp and golden-brown. "Got a pen, Khou?" she called over her shoulder.

"There's two copies for each of you to go through and read before signing," Khouri explained while rummaging in the satchel for a pen.

"No need," Avra said while spreading honey butter on the toast. "I'm ready to sign it now."

"So am I," Sam said, but pushed the contract back across the counter. "Soon as we get back from Kemah."

Setha bit her lip for a second. "It's not very long, Sam. Pretty standard. Y'all should be able to read through it before you leave this afternoon."

"Mmm-hmm…" Sam went to the refrigerator and stared inside for a while. "But like I said, we can't seem to do anything right. I want to change that."

Avra tugged at the wrinkled black T-shirt hanging out over her yoga pants and waited.

"It's part of the agreement that we both go down there to give approval on the shoot." He retrieved a bottle of juice and twisted the cap. "I'd hate for anyone to try backing out of that once the contract is signed and sealed." He took a long swallow of juice.

"You son of a b—!"

"Avra!"

She bowed her head at Khouri's admonishment and then raised apologetic eyes toward Setha. "I didn't mean that. I—I'm sorry." She took her toast and tea from the counter. "Guess I better go get ready. Oh! Khouri?" She set down the food again. "Could I have that pen?" She fielded it easily when he tossed. Quickly, she scribbled her name to both copies of the contract and then threw the pen at Sam's chest.

"You're such a child," she spat.

Setha waited until Avra had been gone from the kitchen for a few seconds. "What the hell happened?" she blurted.

Sam wouldn't respond. With the pen Avra had thrown at him, he signed his name to the contract. He studied the papers for a second and then pulled his sister close and kissed her forehead. Next, he shook hands with Khouri. "Thanks, man." He left the way he came through the back door of the kitchen.

"Do you know what it was they took?" Danilo asked while hunching over his desk.

Basil sat on the other side of the desk as both he and Dan waited for the voice to drift in through the phone's speaker.

"Boxes and crates—tons of 'em carted right out of Tino Viejo's house," a man's voice rumbled.

"Do you know what they have?" Dan repeated the question more pointedly that time.

"Whatever it is, it's got 'em scramblin' and actin' secretive as hell." The man paused to cough. "They've only given a select number of personnel access to it."

Dan massaged his square jaw. "Any way to get to it?"

"Doubtful—they've moved it to some off-site storage. No hint as to where."

"What about this 'select personnel'? You know any of them?" Dan settled down in the chair rubbing his jaw more firmly as he thought. "Is there maybe a way to…encourage one of them to work with us?"

"Sorry, man, I don't have a clue and wouldn't bet on my questioning not raising all kinds of suspicion. I do know that the folks chosen are at the highest level and seem to all run together in the same circle outside the force. Chief of d's ain't takin' no chances."

"Keep at it," Dan instructed and then clicked off the speaker without further conversation. "We need to know what they have."

Basil leaned forward in the chair, resting his elbows to his knees while working fingers into his brow. "You know it could be a lot of nothin'. Tino had to be smart enough not to keep anything like that in his home."

"Yeah, he was smart all right." Dan didn't voice the acknowledgment in a particularly complimentary manner. "I'm guessin' the boy kept all sorts of damaging things and that he kept 'em all over creation."

Basil looked up in time to see Dan grimace and rub a hand across his chest. "Why don't you take a seat?" He left his chair to get a glass of water for his friend.

"Drink," Basil ordered, setting a firm hand to Danilo's shoulder to urge him down into the worn black leather desk chair.

"You know, perhaps Lucas is right," Basil said once Dan downed the glass of water.

"Have you lost your mind?"

"This is all getting away from you too fast," Basil threw back. "It could be worse if you try to run from it. Besides…maybe it's time for it all to come out. You've made your fortune, solidified your legacy for your children and their children. Isn't that enough?"

Still massaging his chest, Dan's expression was grim. "There's no such thing as enough, amigo."

Avra was zipping up the last compartment to the gray overnight bag when a knock fell on her room door.

"Avra?" Setha's voice rang out.

"It's open!"

Avra was tossing the bag to a chair near the closet when she saw Setha walk in carrying a stack of papers. "Forget it." She waved a hand. "I'm not mentioning that contract to Sam. It might be petty, but I'm not giving him the satisfaction of turning me down about signing it."

Setha locked the door and set the folder on the bed. "It's not the contract." Gathering the hem of her sundress, she curled at the foot of the bed. "I know Khouri told you about what I've been looking into—what I found out about Carson Arroyo."

Avra took her place at the head of the bed, tucking her legs beneath her. Slowly, her fingers strayed toward the folder.

"That's everything I was able to pull together and the stuff Carson left in my office when he first came to see me—actually, it was the only time he came to see me there." Setha's fingertips grazed the folder, as well. "Carson's file helped me gather all this other stuff. I'm sorry but nothing really stands out besides what we already know. I thought it might help with the stories you guys were working on at *Ross Review,* though, before Mr. Basil shut all that down."

Setha pushed the folder across the silver comforter. "Khouri's not gonna be easy to deal with if he knows I'm still involved with this."

"And I know Sam doesn't want you thinkin' about this stuff, either," Avra said.

Setha's mouth curved into a soft smile. "My brothers and my dad still don't get how well I can read them." Her voice held on a shrug. "I know this isn't over but I love Khouri too much to keep digging around in it."

Avra scooted forward a bit to squeeze Setha's hand. "And now my dad's stopped all investigation into the murders."

Setha appeared to deflate a bit. "Whatever this is, Av—" she shook her head forebodingly "—it's got the power to affect our families in the worst way. Somebody's gotta find out what it's all about." Decidedly, she pushed the folder directly in front of Avra.

"I'll leave it up to you to decide what to do with it."

She pulled Avra into a hug. "Have fun on the trip," she whispered.

Avra rolled her eyes. "I'd have more fun at a root canal." She cupped Setha's cheek and patted her face gently. "I'll see you when I get back."

"Maybe we should leave him alone. Sooner or later the cops might get around to pinning it on him."

The phone line crackled while silence held it just shy of a full minute.

A second voice joined in the conversation then. "We can't take the risk of the police having more interest in him than they already have. He's hurting and he's angry—a bad combination. Who knows what he'd share in an interrogation room. Handle it with your usual care."

"Yes, sir."

Sam had swiveled his seat toward Avra, who sat next to him in the back of the spacious helicopter. She was sleeping soundly, so he didn't mind shedding the hard expression he'd worn since they left the ranch earlier.

He shook his head, massaging his shoulder blade beneath the navy crew shirt he wore with jeans. The tension there was slow to fade and he wondered how Avra could doze amid the chopper's biting engine. Still, he was grateful that she was unconscious for the moment and indulged in studying her lovely features at rest. The back of his hand trailed her oval face. He recalled the way her skin felt beneath his fingertips when they were under her dress the night before.

Improving her opinion of him at that point was going to be more impossible than it ever was before. Stall-

ing on signing the contract had been an idiotic move.
She was right. He was a child and had only refused to
sign it in front of her as some form of payback for her
turning him away from her bed in *his* house. Travel-
ing to Kemah was the right move. There was too much
going on in Houston. The time away would do them
good even if it was masked behind the cloak of work.

He was rubbing his thumb along her jaw then. By
the time the crew arrived to begin shooting for the
campaign, Avra Ross would acknowledge her feelings
for him and give in to him. He was confident of that.

Sighing then, he ran his hand down her arm, squeezing to rouse her awake. She barely moved at first and
Sam knew it'd take much more to wake someone who
slept so deeply.

Waking her, though, wasn't his utmost priority then.
He wanted her. Sure, it was probably just a physical
need, but something kept nagging at him. It kept unset-
tling him that she'd aroused more than lust, that she was
more than a hobby—a challenge to conquest. Maybe afterward he wouldn't be nearly as obsessed—maybe he
could go longer than a damn hour without thinking of
her. And maybe…maybe he'd be even more obsessed.

Whatever happened, he knew that he wanted her
on the most elemental level. Something would have
to be done about that if he had any hope of discover-
ing whether anything more powerful, more…lasting
lay beyond.

"Avra?" He shook off the thoughts and put more
effort into waking her. "Av?" Squeezing her arms,
bared by the cinched capped sleeves of the empire-
waist blouse, he gave her a tiny shake. Gradually his

big hands worked their way to her hips and thighs, squeezing them interchangeably.

Of course he lost track of his true purpose and the squeezes to her hips and thighs took on a massaging quality.

"Mmm?" Slowly, Avra moved from under the veil of sleep and beneath the spell of something far more provocative.

Long onyx brows drawn close, Sam's attention was riveted to her alluring reaction, which in turn stirred an equally alluring reaction below his waist. He applied a firmer squeeze to her thigh and smiled when she bit her lip and uttered a barely audible whimper.

Her eyes opened and Avra gave a start at finding Sam Melendez on his knees before her.

Reflexively, she inched back on the seat. "Something wrong?"

Sam glanced toward the cockpit. "We're about ready to land. But, um." He took a deep breath and held it for a minute before exhaling. "You're right—something's definitely wrong."

Avra's smile hinted at knowing. "Isn't there always when it comes to us?"

The tease brought something distressed to Sam's expression. As if depleted, he rested his head in her lap.

Instinctively Avra raised her hand intending, *desiring* to trail her fingers through the lush black covering his head. Thinking better of the action, she clenched a fist instead.

"Is there something wrong with the chopper?"

"Oh, um, no, no. I, um—" he dragged a hand back through his hair "—didn't mean to upset you. What's wrong is I didn't apologize for the way I acted this morning."

Avra relaxed into her seat and waited.

Sam read her reaction easily. An apology from him to her was not a usual occurrence.

"I was trying to get back at you for..."

"For last night?" There was no malice in her words. "I wasn't trying to tease you, Sam."

He smirked, lowering his gaze for a moment. "Lady, you could do that by sitting in a chair."

Avra took note of her present stance and her expression reflected pity. "All we'll do is hurt each other, Sam."

"How can you be so sure?"

"Look at our track record, hon."

"That's in business." He rolled his eyes. "We never tried anything more."

"Maybe there isn't any more."

"Do you mind us taking the time to find out?"

She rolled her head against the seat. "I don't play this game well—regardless of what you may think."

He cupped the back of her knee, focusing on his hand there. "What might I be thinkin', darlin'?"

"I know how I come across." She indulged in the sensation stemming from his touch at her knee. "My dad raised me and my sisters to be strong—not to cower before men but to be confident and straightforward about what we want. I take that seriously, more seriously than my sisters maybe."

"You don't trust me, do you?"

"Not with my heart, Sam Melendez."

"Why not me?" His hold firmed at her calf. "I'm sure there're other men you've let..." A muscle flexed dangerously along his jaw. "You've gotten close to other men without giving your heart to them, and that's not me getting the wrong idea. That's me seeing a fantastic woman who wears her sex appeal like a piece of jewelry, knowing a man couldn't resist getting as close as you'd let him." His handsome face was rapt with curiosity.

"Why won't you let me get close, Ms. Ross?"

The chopper pilot's voice rang out in response. "Setting down in five."

When Sam strapped Avra into her seat and moved away, she realized she'd been holding her breath.

Chapter 6

It was close to sunset when the chopper set down in Kemah. The bags were already packed in the Jeep they would take from the airstrip.

"What?" Sam questioned the strange look Avra sent him when he offered to help her down from the aircraft.

"This is new." She squinted slightly against the last remnants of sunlight. "I'm not used to being treated so well by you."

Sam took her hand and helped her from the rail leading off the chopper. He pressed that hand close to his chest. "That's because you never let me."

"Ha! You never *tried,* Sam."

"Maybe you'll let me try now." He pulled her hand from his chest and played with her fingers. "That is, if you're not afraid to let me."

Before she could conjure a reply, Sam let go of her hand and left to speak with the pilot. Closing her eyes, she ordered herself to get it together. The gorgeous setting helped a lot in that regard. Kemah was indeed an enchanted place. Her brother and sister-in-law-to-be had made a great choice of locations.

She was sure there was no real reason for her and Sam to fly down there and give any sort of final approval. Of course it was certainly no hardship to take the trip.

Leaning against the back passenger side of the Jeep, Avra took the time to enjoy the scenery and smiled up at the sky. The changing colors announced the coming of fall. With a sigh she turned to get inside the vehicle and noticed her bags on the backseat. She'd brought along the files Setha had given her.

According to Setha, the notes were in as much disarray as her own. This would perhaps be yet another waste of her time, but Avra knew she'd have to muddle through it anyway. It was about more than curiosity for her. The Melendez murders, her father shutting down the story, even Wade Cornelius's death—it all factored in somehow.

But factored into what? And why was her father so set on keeping them out of it? Was he afraid they'd find something? Was he somehow linked to this?

A door slammed and Avra saw Sam approaching her after leaving the rear compartment of the Jeep.

"Everything okay?" he asked.

She smiled and waved a hand toward the sky. "How could it not be with a view like this?"

"Tell me about it." He leaned next to her against the side of the Jeep.

Together they took in what remained of the sunset.

* * *

Shane Arroyo had played this game long enough to know when a piece had served its purpose and was no longer needed. Whether Carson had realized it or not, he was on borrowed time and would have been taken out of it had he not fallen from a bullet from a cop's gun.

Perhaps he *did* know. Perhaps that's why he made such an idiotic move in approaching Setha Melendez at a public event the way he had. One last hurrah to get her to see the ugly foundation on which her family's beautiful lifestyle rested.

"Yeah, they would have killed you, *hermano*. Just like they'll kill me."

Shane knew that part of the plan was in the works and probably had been part of the game from the very start. Perhaps he and his brother had been brought into this as expendable pawns. After all, their interest in taking down Danilo Melendez was personal. Business played a very small role.

Shane felt pressure behind his eyes and pressed the back of his hand across his face. He was surprised to find moisture clinging to his skin and studied it but a moment. He shook off whatever the sight of tears was doing to him and continued backing the label for the box he was about to ship to his mother.

"Setha said something about a nice inn." Avra warily eyed the forty-foot vessel in her line of sight.

"It's not as nice as a stateroom on my boat," Sam countered.

Again, Avra observed the yacht. "It'll just be the two of us?"

"That a problem for you?"

"Depends on your ability to handle this thing."

"Well, not that I'm trying to brag—"

"'Course not."

"My navigational skills are near expert," he continued with an air that was playfully indignant. "I've been handling boats since I was ten."

Avra nodded. "Impressive."

Sam studied her, his dark eyes fallen into heavier shadow given the night. "Impressive enough for you not to give me a hard time about staying here?" His voice was soft.

Avra couldn't have done that had she wanted to. The short trip to where Sam's boat was docked had worn her out in spite of the nap she'd taken on the helicopter.

"I need to turn in anyway." She yawned.

"You need to eat. I'll give you two hours, then I'll come get you for supper." He moved closer to intentionally crowd her. "I'd appreciate it if you wouldn't argue with me."

Waving her hands in compliance, she headed up the dock. *Samson's Delilah* was almost as stunning as the Kemah sunset had been—almost. Still, it held Avra speechless as she walked the starboard deck. She trailed her fingertips along the wood-grain railings that were trimmed in bronze and ran the length of the black vessel.

"Just had to get your name on it somehow," Avra noted, eyeing the ship's nameplate and shaking her head.

"Don't hate me for being vain." Sam let the straps from the bags slide from his shoulders. "Besides, this way I don't have to worry about upsetting a lovely lady by not having *her* name plastered on the paneling."

"This way—" Avra reached for the strap of her bag and pulled it close "—one of your many *lovely ladies* can fancy herself as being your Delilah."

"No, Av, that could only be one woman." His demeanor was serious then.

"Humph." She stifled her desire to laugh outright. "And the woman who believes that is a fool."

"You're a hard-ass."

Groaning then, Avra covered her face with both hands. "Most of it's the sleepiness talkin'."

"I think I know what those numbers are," he said next, having watched her steadily for a few moments. "The ones in Cornelius's notes."

She leaned against the rail and waited.

Sam followed suit against an opposite railing. "Street number to the address the victims all shared."

"Of course…" She sighed, worrying the collar of her blouse. "14918 Figueroa Trail. Do you know it?"

"I don't think I've ever been there."

Avra heard his deep voice catch and tilted her head. "But?"

Sam was the one to hide his face in his hands that time. "Got a scary feelin' I've seen it."

"Seen it." Her voice was flat. "Seen the address?" When he nodded, she smiled. "I must be sleepier than I thought." His response made no sense to her.

Taking pity on her confusion, Sam pushed off the railing. "Let me show you to your room."

"Think I can find it myself?"

He grinned. "Still don't trust me, huh?"

She tugged on the strap of her bag. "Keep sharin' info and that may change."

"In what way?" His roguish gaze raked her body in a way that left no doubt as to the *way* he preferred.

"Should I lock my door, Sam?"

"Ah, Av…" He dropped an arm across her shoulders in a gesture of camaraderie. "There're no locks on my doors. I'm an open book."

"And the woman who believes *that* is a fool." Avra sighed.

Once Samson left Avra in her cabin, she found that she was too keyed up to simply fall back into sleep mode. The revelation about the address prompted her to take another look at the Cornelius file. She paid special attention to all the places the address showed up in Wade's story notes. Her eyes narrowed when she observed a note on one of the pages that she'd barely scanned before.

"'See V.H. 9, 18, 97,'" she murmured, brushing her fingers across the scrawl. "9, 18, 97," she repeated in bewilderment until realization dawned about what appeared to be a simple date.

"Come in!" she called when Sam knocked.

"Did you even get thirty minutes in?" he asked, frowning at the papers littering the queen bed.

Avra was shuffling through other pages then. "Did you really expect me to sleep after what you told me?"

"I did. You're gonna need your rest, trust me."

Avra ordered herself not to look at him. The tone of his words was suggestive enough.

"9, 18, 97." She spoke the date instead, moving some

of the papers aside when Sam came over to take a seat near the foot of the bed.

He shrugged. "What about it?"

"Wade had a meeting with Vita Arroyo that day."

Sam's dark eyes lowered to the spot she pointed to on a sheet of paper. Then he pressed a thumb to his dimpled chin and grinned. "Are we forgetting our ABCs?"

"The meeting had to be before she changed her last name."

"Avra, those letters could stand for anything."

"They don't." She shook her head stubbornly. "I know for a fact that he was meeting Vita Arroyo."

Her surety sobered him. "How?"

"When he left that day to see her, I asked if I could tag along. Watch him in action. I used to love those field trips." She settled back against the pillow-lined headboard and reminisced.

Sam's gaze slid across her body with blatant deliberateness, blatant desire. The chiseled angles of his handsome face softened some as he watched her remembering the mentor she adored. His eyes continued to trail her form curled on the tangled bed. He realized he was staring before she did and faked studying one of the papers sprinkled across the rose-blush comforter.

"He told me it wasn't a meeting he could take me on—that my dad wouldn't like it. I told him—argued with him, actually—about how much Daddy supported our working together. I went on and on about how much I'd learned already…" She grimaced and nudged one of the papers with her bare foot. "He wouldn't budge and I got all full of myself as I often did."

"Nooo…. You?"

Avra used her bare foot to bump Sam's thigh. "I told Wade all he wanted was to show me how to interview people for garden parties and voter-registration drives… I accused him of drawing the line at letting me get any real experience with important stories." She drew her knees up to her chin and hugged herself. "He said he didn't have time to argue with me then, grabbed his stuff and said somethin' about how lucky he was that *Mrs. Holloway* had even agreed to meet with him. Everybody knew the name Holloway since John Holloway had died—"

"Two years earlier," Sam finished.

Her smile was without humor. "I didn't give up. I kept at him about it. Finally he said he could get fired for even looking into it. Dad didn't want the *Review* following up on anything about that family. He said he wouldn't do anything to put himself more at odds with my dad. Then he left." Her expressive brown eyes carried a haunting quality then. "It was the last time we spoke."

"Ever?" Sam's frown was deep.

Avra nodded. "The next day Wade and Daddy got into this big fight—everybody in the building knew about it." She tucked her bare feet beneath her jean-clad thighs. "I took the day off—pouting because of the way Wade dismissed me. After the fight with Dad…I couldn't even get Wade to talk to me on the phone and then he left Houston for a while… We fell out of touch. When he came back—" she could feel tears pressing against her eyes "—I never reached out."

Sam's expression reflected sympathy and he reached out to squeeze the foot that once again lay closer to his thigh.

"You were just trying to be loyal—respectful of your father's wishes."

"And that cost me one of my dearest friends."

"Yeah." His thumb began a slow massage at the arch of her foot. "I do know what that's like."

"We were fresh out of college then." Avra settled deeper into the pillows. "Old enough to comprehend the rumors about John Holloway's death. I sure did get an earful from my Mass Communications classmates about slanted reporting and how *Ross Review* was a prime example of that in its handling of the facts regarding Melendez involvement or...responsibility for the man's firing and the consequences of that." She bit her thumbnail and risked looking at him then. "Didn't you ever ask your dad about it?"

"Me and my brothers knew better than to mention the Holloway name around the house." Sam worked his fingers over a heavily chorded forearm that was bared beneath the short sleeve of his crew shirt. "To this day, I've never brought him up in my dad's presence." Some unnamed emotion dimmed his gaze then. "Not much scares me, Av, but if that man put his mind to it, he could probably make me wet my pants."

Avra's sudden laughter was a welcome bright spot amid the rather glum mood. Sam quickly celebrated his ability to rouse the gesture from her.

"So now can I persuade you to take a break?" He moved from the bed. "Steaks lose something if they sit around for too long."

Avra didn't hesitate to nod, happy to be leaving behind Wade's notes and the dismal memories they invoked. She accepted Samson's hand when he offered it and together they left the cabin.

* * *

"In here." Shane Arroyo watched the shadow fill the den door and then he smiled at the man it belonged to. "I was hoping the old man would've come to see me himself."

"You knew that wouldn't happen. I'm sorry about this, Shane."

"Save it." Shane snorted. "I've known you long enough to know how smart you are—how calculating."

"Why, thank you, Shane."

"Don't mention it." Shane ignored the sarcasm. "I'm guessing you hoped the cops would come knockin' on my door with handcuffs." Shane smiled, reading the confirmation on the man's face. "But the old man wants me dead."

"He's worried, Shane. He's waited a long time to put this together—can't risk it fallin' apart like this."

"Right. That's the way it's always been so I'm not surprised. This thing fallin' apart is how this whole mess got started." Shane resituated himself in the recliner. "That's why he brought Carson into this—to kill those who refused to help him bring down Dan Melendez. Those kids were a risk. They may have run to the cops or worse—to Melendez himself and told him what was coming down. And now it's my turn." He sighed.

The man in the doorway pulled a gun wearing a silencer from the valise he carried. "I'm sorry about this," he said.

Seconds later two shots whispered into the air and Shane Arroyo lay dead.

Chapter 7

"Well, well, Sam, I didn't know you had it in you."

"Told you to give me a chance."

Avra smiled while surveying the spread of food Samson had prepared. A square table on the deck was filled with four dishes.

"I wouldn't have pegged you for a cook," she said, breaking off a roll and savoring the taste. "Many things, but never a cook."

"Man's gotta eat." Sam held a chair for her.

"True." Avra took her place. "But the son of Danilo Melendez has people to cook *for* him, right?"

"Very few people cook as well as I do." Sam's tone was matter-of-fact. "Even my dad can't deny my skills and it was pretty hard for him to admit I had any."

"Hard because you're being groomed to run MM?"

"Hard because I was a son instead of a daughter."

a nibbled her biscuit slowly then. Her brown eyes
ed Sam while he paced the deck's gleaming sur-
his bare feet as he listened to the caller.
ght...I understand, yeah." He tossed the phone to
the cushioned navy blue seats along the side of
t. For a time he stood deep in thought, working
mb into the dimple in his chin. He felt Avra's
ring into him and turned.
ne Arroyo's dead—murdered."
's hands flew to her open mouth.
watched the shivers overcome her. He wasted
coming to kneel before her once he'd tugged
r around to face him.
ped it was Carson—" her voice was soft, vir-
ildlike "—but then when he died I thought
could've been his brother trying to get re-
Melendez firing his dad and us for reporting
w he's dead."
"
's next, Sam?"
Avra?" He pulled her trembling hands into
, covering them easily. "You stop this, all
right?" He gave her hands a firm shake.
nna figure this out, darlin'. Don't you worry."
She blinked against the tears clinging to her
muttered a curse at the display of emotion.
oothed his free hand along her bare arm.
t we start with the best lead we have. My

uddered. "What are we gonna find if we
g in this, Sam?"
He squeezed her thigh and stood. "Finish
turned the heavy chair she occupied back

"Ah." Avra propped her chin in her palm. "And tough guys don't cook."

Sam shrugged and reached for the wine.

"Guess it's not easy being the son of a powerful man."

"It's not easy being the *oldest* son of a powerful man."

Avra leaned over to let him fill her glass with the full-bodied Merlot. "Ah, yes...the demands of the first-born. Will the talents of the parents be passed down, blah, blah, blah..."

"Damn right." Sam poured the wine and then used the bottle opener for the beer he had chilling. "Not an easy life, 'specially after my mother died."

"I can relate." Her tone barely registered. She sipped the wine, letting it rest on her tongue for a moment before she swallowed.

"Yeah...raisin' little sisters is no joke," Sam noted with a grin.

"Neither is raising little brothers."

"Amen!" he bellowed.

Avra raised her glass in a toast. "You did a very fine job with your little sister."

"And you, as well, with Khouri," Sam said after accepting her compliment with a humble nod.

They enjoyed their drinks in silence then looking out at the Kemah lights from their places on deck. Shortly, though, Sam was moving to prepare their plates.

"I think I know that address. The one the victims shared," he added when he saw her watching him blankly.

"You've been there?"

"No, but I think I've seen it."

* * *

"Who found him?" Chief Bradley Crest stood in a small circle of uniformed and plainclothes officers and looked down on the body of Shane Arroyo.

"Nosy landlord," one of the officers said. "He didn't see the perp's face but saw him leavin'. The idiot yelled out and the guy started runnin'."

"Lucky him." Brad grimaced while shaking his head.

"Landlord knocked," the officer continued. "When there was no answer, he decided to check it out—found him."

Brad shifted his grimace toward his first lieutenant. "Think we'll find a damn lead this time?"

"A lead, boss?" Gregory Roth appeared stumped.

"Greg, the man's brother was just killed—"

"Well, boss…I mean there could be *some* connection but his brother died in the course of trying to leave with Setha Melendez. He was killed, not murdered."

"Still too much coincidence." Brad scratched the hair at his nape. "I want to know everything about this guy."

"What're we lookin' for, boss?"

Brad's blue eyes made a cursory inspection of Shane Arroyo's body. "Anything," he said.

"Remember the painting in my den?"

"The mural?" Avra's brows drew close. "The one drawn from the photo my dad took?"

Sam nodded slow, tapping the mouth of the beer bottle to his jaw. "I've only seen the picture a few times. Back when I was havin' the mural done." He set down the beer to cut a sliver from his rib eye. "There was

writing on the back—Figueroa Tr ber the number, but if my guess place else out there."

Avra's back was straight—she seat. "Why would Wade have the Why were all the victims there?

Sam watched her intently, the was deep in thought.

"Do you know how to get th

Avra's question roused a gr He began to bump his fist agai ert from the looks of that pict not enough to narrow it down

"And I'm guessin' you're dad about it?"

"No more than you are to

Avra took part in the "gr dad who took the picture." on the table and pressed the forehead.

"Are you saying you'll a food but was more interest

A cell phone's ring pierc decide.

"That you?" Sam aske hands woefully.

"Haven't seen my cell Probably left it at home.

Sam wiped his mout to his plate and then we smiled and reached for curse at the realization answered lightly at fir toward the table. Before returning to his seat, he placed a hard, lingering kiss into the top of her curls and murmured something sweet yet indecipherable.

Later that night Brad Crest was in his office reviewing notes on the case. He'd been in deep concentration close to forty minutes when Gregory Roth walked in wearing one of his grim expressions.

"Spill it," Brad ordered, eyeing the file folder Greg had brought to the office with him.

"This is that ugly stuff I was tellin' you about."

"Well, don't prolong it." Brad tossed a pen onto the hodgepodge of papers on the coffee table.

"Martino Viejo was embezzling funds from the very organizations he'd helped build." Greg opened the file, laying it flat on the counter across the office. "Those journals we took from his house were ledgers dating back over ten years. He wasn't helping himself to much." Greg rubbed his slightly pointed chin while reading from the file. "Guess that's sayin' somethin' given the amount of charities he oversaw, but a little adds up to be a lot since he was dippin' out of all of 'em."

"Dammit." Brad's muttered word seemed to echo in the room.

"Boss, um—" Greg rubbed his chin a little more intently as though he were debating with himself "—maybe you might want to take time from this. I know how close to home this hits with the Melendezes being friends and all."

"Can we pin this murder or any of the others on Melendez?"

Greg's wrinkled blue dress shirt wrinkled a bit more

when he shrugged. "Anything's possible, boss. It's a pretty big company—gonna take a lot to establish links between the vics to anyone at MM. If there *are* any links to be made, that is…"

"Greg," Brad groaned and for a while hid his face in his hands. "I'm not asking whether you can pin this on Melendez the company but Melendez the man."

Some of the color drained from Greg's face. "You mean…Dan Melendez?"

"The one and only."

Greg groped for the dark-cushioned chair behind him and took a seat. "You really like him for this?"

In silence Brad reflected on the night he'd told Sam Melendez and his father about the Viejo murder. Dan looked as if he'd been hit in the gut with a wrecking ball. Of course his reaction could have been due to the shock of losing a valuable employee. But what if it was more than that? Brad had been a cop almost twenty years and had learned enough by now to know not to ignore his hunches. Something was telling him that Dan Melendez's involvement in the murders went beyond him simply being the employer of a growing list of dead employees.

"Keep this quiet," he said to Greg, who'd been watching him expectantly. "I want you to sniff down this path till you come to a dead end."

Dinner between Sam and Avra continued in easy quiet aside from the occasional clink of glasses or silverware.

"Guess this'll be our last time working together," Sam noted from his reclining position in the chair he occupied. His midnight eyes held a guarded intensity as he watched her top off her coffee.

"You're forgetting we'll have to meet up to renew the annual agreement."

"I don't want to wait that long." He lowered his gaze.

"Sam." She focused on her coffee. "Don't—"

"Why do you think I brought you out here?"

The alluring line of her mouth curved into a smile. "Business," she drawled.

Sam wasn't amused. "You're not a stupid woman," he said.

Avra pushed her chair back from the table and stood. "I think I'm done here. You want me to do the dishes?"

He barely lifted a hand. "I got it." He didn't bother to look her way.

Regret pooled the bottomless brown of her stare and she dismissed it fast. "I'm gonna go look over some stuff before bed, then." She turned on her heel and made for the staircase leading down to the quarters. She was halfway there when her steps would carry her no farther.

"Sam...I—"

"Save it."

Avra waited. His words stirred the harsh twinge of regret again. After a moment or two, her feet cooperated and she left the deck.

In her cabin Avra didn't bother changing into night-clothes, but cracked right into the file Setha had given to her earlier that day. She'd kicked off her socks and sneakers and sat with her legs folded on the bed while she massaged her feet.

It had been such a long day. There had been so

many revelations and they'd come at her from every damn angle. Especially Sam. What he suggested was crazy talk after all the time they'd spent at each other's throats. It could never work.

Stubbornly, Avra shook her head at the voice that asked if she wasn't even the tiniest bit curious about what he was like in bed. Now especially after all the brief encounters he'd treated her to as of late.

"Dammit, girl…concentrate." She whipped open the thick file folder of notes. Hungrily, she scanned a wealth of information and nodded in recognition. Much of what Setha had uncovered, she'd found in Wade's notes.

With some items that merited a closer look, Avra moved from the bed and sat at the rolltop desk in the corner. Over the next ten or twelve minutes she sat there and categorized the information. One stack was for material that matched things she'd already uncovered. Another was for things requiring further research. The last stack she'd labeled miscellaneous. That stack included pictures she'd found along with a few maps. The pictures occupied her complete attention.

The snapshots were obviously quite dated, with the kind of hazy beige tint pictures tended to adopt over time. Some were landscape photos—desert area given the vast flatness, sand and tumbleweeds in many of the shots. Others were pictures of old cars—70s models; a few were snaps of people.

To those, Avra paid special attention. Her delicate features sharpened as she frowned while peering closely at the faces of the men, women and even children that smiled shyly into the camera.

It was a group shot that stopped her, yet quickened

the pace of her heart. Another few seconds of studying the picture had her mouth falling open.

There was a single, booming knock to the door, which opened before Avra could give Sam permission to enter. She didn't mind, since she wanted to tell him what she'd discovered and suspected.

She was standing from the desk and preparing to follow through on that when Sam took her elbow and dipped his dark head to kiss her. Naturally, she melted, a given reaction whenever he touched her. Eagerly, her tongue fought back against his. She forgot everything until he backed her against the rolltop. Then, she recalled the pictures.

"Sam…wait…"

He only grunted something incomprehensible while increasing the pressure of the kiss. He alternated between exploring her mouth and heatedly pressing his persuasive lips against hers.

"Sam…" She tried again *barely* to reach him.

He responded by hefting her slight form against his broad chest. Wide palms cradling her bottom, Sam crossed the cabin and settled her on the middle of the bed.

Avra gave in to the act, relishing the roughness of his tongue as it massaged her own. His hands were providing an equally stunning massage to her bottom while pressing her into his breath-stealing arousal.

"Sam, wait a minute." She paused, needing to catch her breath when he left off kissing her to relieve her of the blouse.

"We need to talk." She practically moaned the words, unable to add any more force to them. "Listen to me, dammit." Those words were barely a whisper.

Sam lifted her and peeled the blouse from her back. "It's important…"

With a deft, intent touch, he unfastened her bra and tugged at the garment with a bit more insistence than he'd used with the blouse. He barely had her out of it when his gorgeous, copper-toned face was nestled between her small, full breasts.

Avra was quickly losing whatever will she may've had to resist. She allowed herself to enjoy the feel of his large, muscular frame sheltering her. The pleasurable mastery of his lips and tongue feasting on her cleavage was undeniable. Intermittently, he encircled a nipple and then returned to barely nibble the bud.

Avra was mad with need by the time he moved on to the second breast. Restless, she buried her hands in her short, glossy curls while arching more of her body into his mouth.

When Sam was satisfied by the pout of the nipples, he moved lower. His mouth spanned her rib cage and belly button, which he treated to a brief tongue kiss.

"Sam, listen to me." She gasped the halfhearted plea. "Listen to me…" She heard a low growl rise from the vicinity of her waist where he was busy unfastening her jeans.

"Later" was his only reply.

Chapter 8

Naked beneath the man who had been her nemesis for far too long, Avra forgot about trying to get him to listen to her. Instead, she set out to remove his shirt but he took her wrists with one hand and held them between her breasts. With his free hand he tossed her jeans and underwear over the side of the bed and began a devastating assault on her sex.

The unexpected treat had her bucking wildly beneath him in seconds. Sam let go of her wrists, tugging them down to rest at her hips, where he lay between her legs. Large hands eased beneath her thighs and hooked over the tops to keep her secure on the bed and open to whatever he wanted.

In spite of the commanding hold, Avra tried to move. She couldn't resist grabbing on to the slightest ability to rotate her hips in response to the erotic moves of his kiss inside her body. Her breath came in brisk pants when he tongued the moist petals of her core and then nibbled the satiny coffee-brown folds of skin there before thrusting briefly, deeply, hotly.

"Sam." Her voice carried a pleading chord. She pleaded then, however, for a completely different reason, wanting to sob as desire ripped through her.

Quickly, she reached the point where his tongue was simply *not* hitting the spot that ached desperately for his touch. Only one part of his body was capable of doing that…and more…

"Sam…" She tried to nudge her upper thighs against his cheeks in an effort to urge him on to other things. She felt his breath cooling her heated skin when he shushed her.

"Patience, Ms. Ross…"

Avra could have obliged had she at least been able to drape her legs across his powerful shoulders. Had she the freedom to wind her hips as he feasted on her, she may've been able to exercise a *bit* more patience.

Sam was having none of that. He'd wanted her too long and had the nerve to make the first move. Besides, her cries in the air as he pleasured her were a stimulant his ego wasn't quite ready to let go of yet. He drove his tongue deeper then, his grin shielded by her thighs when she cried out.

"Sam, Sam, take this off." Her nails were curled into his shirt as she yanked the material insistently. "Let me see you."

He was willing to meet that request. Her lashes fluttered apart when she felt him rise above her. She watched him grab the shirt at the back of his neck and tug it over his head. Heavy tendrils of straight, dark hair fell across his brow as he did so.

Avra started to rotate against the tousled covers. She ground her hips on one of his massive denim-clad thighs. She was just that affected by the sight of the toned beauty before her eyes.

To say his chest was broad was an understatement. Being tentative wasn't something Avra was accustomed to, but it was definitely her reaction when she reached out to test the power of his build.

She bit her lip when her hand settled against a pec and kneaded lightly as she took note of the definition of his body. His torso seemed unreal, she thought while tracing the perfectly cut muscles that made up his abdomen. She spread both hands across the broad, copper-toned plane while grinding herself on his thighs in a more insistent fashion.

Sam brought his mouth back to her breast; ravenously he suckled and growled when the nipples firmed again at his manipulation. He settled over her, but kept the brunt of his weight rested on his fists planted on either side of her hips.

Avra didn't want delicate handling. She scraped her nails down his back, tracing the muscles flexing there beneath her touch. Her hands drifted downward, curving over his butt to draw him fully down atop her.

"Wait…dammit, Av…"

She couldn't resist smiling at the concern clinging to his rough, deep voice. A measure of triumph rushed inside her over the mere possibility of wielding any power over the man after all their previous run-ins. How much she'd despised him and how much he'd seemed to despise her. For them to meet on this level, needy with desire, yes, but also emotionally connecting… She could never have expected that would occur between them.

"I'm fine." She dragged her lips down the heavily corded length of his neck. "I'm fine…"

"I don't want to hurt you," he murmured even as he settled more of his weight on her slender frame.

Avra tunneled her hands through his hair, sighing as the silky strands slid between her fingers.

Sam lost what little restraint he was trying to hang on to. He'd so wanted to prolong the night, but he'd have her again. Of that he was sure. He'd have her many times again. Mindlessly, he began to kiss his way down her svelte dark frame while undoing his jeans fastening. Impatiently, he kicked away the denims.

"Dammit, Sam," Avra hissed when his mouth left her.

"Hush," he softly ordered.

Avra's next reply was a breathless groan. His thumb was applying a wicked massage to the extrasensitive bud of sensation at the apex of her thighs. She rested her arms above her head, toying in her hair while rotating her hips and shuddering on the pleasure stemming from his fingers.

Sam's pitch stare was riveted on her lovely dark face as he enjoyed the sight of her enjoying his touch. He looked away just long enough to reach for protection from the back pocket of the jeans he'd kicked aside.

"No…" Avra pouted when he stopped touching her. Her voice was just silencing when he returned with protection in place.

In one swift move he had her off her back and straddling his lap once he'd kneeled in the middle of the bed. One hand captured her chin, angling her for his kiss as the other clutched her bottom and easily settled her down to sheath his erection.

Avra buried her nails into his shoulders and moaned shakily during the kiss. She would have tossed back her head, but Sam wasn't letting her break the kiss. He merely deepened it, making it hotter, wetter. When he was satisfied that she was a complete participant, he released her chin to cradle her derriere in both hands. Avra didn't dare break the kiss but gasped several times in the midst of it.

He handled her effortlessly, sensually lifting her from his sex and resettling her with a slow devastation that forced a myriad of sounds from her mouth.

Avra couldn't keep her head up and let it rest on his shoulder. Sobs escaped her into his skin where she softly bit down after each thrust he subjected her to. Only moments later, she took control and shoved him to his back where she rode him slow for a while.

It was Sam gasping *her* name then in ragged pants. He kept a loose hold on her hips and then let go all together, pressing the heels of his hands into his eyes and groaning without shame.

Avra knew she was seconds away from total satisfaction and prayed Sam was close for she didn't know whether she had the strength or desire to wait. She added more speed to her ride, grazing his chest with her nails. She flicked them across his nipples before soaking them with her tongue when she leaned close.

Sam tightened his hold on her hips and lunged up into her with such force, Avra climaxed in the next moment. Sam's ebony gaze was narrowed and steady as he studied her in the throes of orgasm. His own release came when she cupped her breasts and threw back her head to moan over what he was doing to her.

Silently, Sam repeated the earlier promise he'd made

to himself. He would have her many times again. He'd thought of making her his for too long. Now that he had her, he didn't imagine himself letting go of her anytime soon. Anytime…ever.

Following two more devastating love sessions, Sam and Avra dozed off and on into the wee hours of the morning.

"This is gonna put a serious chink in our working relationship." Avra sighed, drowsiness still claiming her voice.

Sam gathered her close to him and hid his face in her short crop of unruly curls. "How so?" His voice held the same drowsy undercurrent.

Avra took her time producing an answer. She was far more interested in following the path of her hand across his broad chest.

"Don't worry, it's a nice chink," she said finally. "It could still be a problem, though."

Sam shifted, tugging her more securely atop him. "How so?" he asked.

She outlined the dimple in his chin. "Nobody's gonna know what to think if we suddenly start being nice to each other."

Samson's hearty chuckling shook his big body. His gaze narrowed a bit more then as he appraised her face. "I don't mind fighting in public, so long as we're good to each other in private." He cradled her bottom through the covers and tugged her up to meet his kiss.

Avra moaned, beginning a subtle grind of her hips to his firming and lengthening sex. "How long do you think we can stand that? Being nice to each other?"

"Would it make you mad if I said I'd rather speculate on other things?"

Avra could feel the persistent thud of her heart beating beneath her breast and knew he could feel it, too. Her eyelids grew heavy in response to him squeezing and clutching her rump.

"What would you rather speculate on?" she whispered.

Sam gnawed the satiny column of her neck where faint traces of her perfume still lingered. Without warning, he flipped her to her back. "How many times I can make you scream when I'm inside you."

Avra let her lashes flutter in an exaggerated fashion while sliding her hands up along the sinewy length of his biceps. "That's a tall order," she drawled.

"I can handle it."

"Hmm?" She scrunched her nose dubiously. "I don't know...I've been told I'm a hard-ass."

Sam had worked his way down to outline her collarbone with the tip of his tongue. Then his handsome face disappeared between her breasts. "I think I can handle you," he boasted amid licking, outlining and suckling her nipples.

"Do you, now?" She arched her back. "I'd love to see you try."

"Hell, woman, haven't I proved that over the past five and a half hours?"

"Mmm...I have a tendency to forget."

"Let's see what I can do about that." He cupped both her breasts then and alternated between attending to her nipples.

Avra rested her hands above her head and arched her back more directly. Sam skimmed the undersides of her breasts with his mouth and then his nose. Soon he'd disappeared beneath the tangle of bedcovers.

Shortly afterward Avra felt herself being pulled down toward the center of the bed. Sam situated her so that her legs were over his shoulders but atop the covers. The position left the part of her that he craved open for feasting. Avra placed her hands over the comforter where his head moved.

Under the covers Sam was aroused by the smell of his body on hers. He'd spent the better part of the night putting it there. He had a ways to go before he was done, though. A smell could be washed away. He wanted to be inside her in every way—wanted to be on her mind and often.

His lips spanned the silken petals of her center. He nudged them apart using his nose and then his fingers and then took her with his tongue.

Above the covers Avra delighted in every thrust and rotation that claimed her. In the midst of it all, she squeezed her eyes shut to ward off the familiar voice that hinted softly that their bliss wouldn't last. She didn't need to think about that. She realized that. Good things weren't in the cards for her and Samson Melendez.

Her gasping nudged into moaning when he put his fingers to work with his tongue. Well…some things were good, she decided.

She feared that they weren't, unfortunately, the good things necessary for a lengthy relationship. She shook her head slowly against the pillows then. *Relationship* was definitely not in the cards for her and Sam. It was only sex. Just… She left off thinking, on the verge of climax.

It was just exquisite, fabulous sex and that was quite good enough for her. She could hear Sam grunting beneath the covers as his feasting turned hungrier. Blindly Avra reached out toward the night table. She fumbled about until she clutched one of the condoms Sam had tossed there earlier. She slid it beneath the covers and smiled when his teeth closed over the package.

Chapter 9

"Once again from our Houston desk, Martino Viejo, Community Relationships VP for Machine Melendez, was found shot dead. Sources say the wound was not self-inflicted. Back to you, Spencer..."

"Ah, damn..." Avra groaned, holding the coffeepot poised over a mug while she listened to the television news broadcast.

Sam didn't look up from the eggs he cracked into a glass bowl. "Knew that would get out to the surrounding areas soon. Won't be long till the rest of the country knows what kind of storm we've got brewin' down here."

Avra filled her mug and then turned her back on the small TV mounted above the double sink in the spacious galley. "You really think it'll go that far?" She stirred the coffee slowly, watching as the cream she'd added turned the liquid to a light beige.

Sam set aside the glass bowl and then dragged both hands through his hair. "Do you know Brad Crest?"

"Chief of Detectives Brad Crest?" Avra nodded. "Why?"

"He's been keepin' me in the know about this thing from the jump. Made a trip out to the ranch to tell us about Viejo. My dad almost fainted when he heard."

Avra sipped her coffee without really tasting it.

Sam leaned against the cooking island and folded his arms across his bare chest while staring down at his feet. "My dad couldn't have hidden that reaction had he tried. Brad noticed... Man's a good cop." He brought his eyes up to meet Avra's. "If he's not already investigating my father, he will be soon. That alone is cause for national attention and *that* won't be good for us businesswise—it'll be even worse if they actually find something."

"What do you think they'll find?"

Sam offered an abrupt laugh. "Hell, that address for one."

"And what do you think they'll find there?"

"I don't know." Sam massaged his eyes and his shoulders appeared to hunch a bit. "But if it was anything good it damn sure wouldn't be hidden away like it seems to be."

Avra brought the mug to her mouth and held it there. A second later she set it to the counter and ran from the galley.

"Somethin' I said?" Sam was asking when Avra returned in the span of a few minutes. He was scrambling eggs then, holding a large iron skillet over two plates.

Avra placed the folder she'd brought to the table and then went to the stove.

"Go sit," she ordered Sam, motioning for him to pass her the skillet. "Take a look at that." She nodded toward the photo she'd put atop the folder.

Sam did as he was told and Avra finished the eggs. Slouching in the seat, he studied the photo disinterestedly. Other than the worn quality of the shot, nothing really stood out to him.

"Look at the scenery," Avra instructed, spooning out the fluffy yellow eggs between two deep green ceramic plates.

"Son of a…" Sam muttered less than a second later. "Where'd you get this?"

"Setha." Avra set the empty pan on a back burner. "She gave me everything she found when she was trying to look into this on her own. She told me to use what I could to find what answers I could."

"This is the same place from my mural—from the picture your dad took. How'd my sister get it?" His deep voice was monotone.

"Carson Arroyo."

"Arroyo…" Sam continued to study the photo, massaging the square bend of his jaw as he did so. "What do you know?" he asked her.

Avra set the heavy plates on the silverware. "Look at the people in the photo." She scooped the eggs into her mouth while Sam did what she told him. "There's a mix of kids and adults."

The beginnings of a frown tugged at Sam's sleek brows. "Am I supposed to know 'em?"

"I do, at least two of 'em anyway." She swallowed her eggs then wiped her hands to a napkin and leaned over the table. She pointed to a man and woman to the left of the top row.

"Vita Arroyo and Lucas Anton," she said.

A full-blown frown darkened Sam's face then and he watched Avra as if she had two heads. Then his black stare shifted back to the picture. "You're sure?" he breathed.

"I've met Vita." Avra settled back to her eggs. "She's in her fifties but doesn't look a day older than she is in that photo. Lucas Anton used to visit my dad at the *Review* a lot. Especially in the heyday of all the fluff pieces on MM. I haven't seen him in a long time, but I do know that face in the picture."

Sam tapped the photo on the tabletop. "What're you thinkin'?"

"I'd love to know what that address is and why my father was there."

Sam brought his fingers to his temples and sighed. "Me, too."

Setha used her hand to shield her eyes from the bright, rejuvenating sunlight spilling down and drenching the ranch in gold. She stood near a high fence and watched as a group of wranglers worked to lead a hulking bull into a stall. Her attention was rapt on the scene when a pair of arms eased about her waist. She leaned back, inhaling the fantastic cologne that drifted beneath her nose.

"Mmm…my fiancé's not a guy to play with. He won't like finding me in another man's arms."

"He knows you're impossible to resist. I think he'll understand." Khouri's voice was slightly muffled while he spoke into Setha's neck.

She turned in his hold and, moving to her toes, kissed him deep.

"So what's up?" Khouri asked once their heated exchange had drawn to an end.

"Preparations for Sam's annual rodeo." Setha looked over her shoulder at the uncooperative bull. She turned back to Khouri when she heard him laughing. "What?"

"A rodeo and a wedding."

Setha had to laugh then, too.

"I hope your brother can handle my sister better than these guys are handlin' this bull," he mused.

"Oh…I don't think Sam'll mind letting her win out over him."

"So you don't think they're getting into it every five minutes?" Khouri leaned against the fence to observe the wranglers and the black steer.

"I bet they're getting along just *fine*." Setha resumed her spot along the fence. "They've only got each other for company."

"Humph, better the devil you know, huh?"

"Somethin' like that." Setha shook windblown tendrils of hair from her eyes and smiled. "Besides, the ad crew will be down there soon. That'll take some of the pressure off."

"Let's hope so."

"Well, I don't think it'll be necessary." Setha nudged Khouri's unyielding shoulder. "Like I said, I get the feeling they're getting along just fine."

The bath inside the master cabin was steamy and alive with the sounds of pleasure. Avra's handprint was smeared into the moisture beaded across the mirror. She braced on that hand while the other curved about

Sam's forearm where he braced his fists on either side of her hips.

Locked in the embrace, they enjoyed one another on the black marble countertop. Sam rested his forehead in the crook of Avra's neck while keeping his thrusts strong and constant.

"Am I hurting you?" he asked when her passionate cries carried on a higher octave.

"I'll kill you if you stop," she gasped.

Sam grinned but didn't stop the lunges that had him less than a minute away from release. He pulled Avra off the counter, yet kept her sealed to his erection.

As he claimed her with renewed intensity, Avra sobbed her pleasure into his broad chest. Lightly she slammed her fist against it as he manipulated her movements along his wide, stiff length. They peaked almost in unison and remained in the embrace to enjoy the lingering effects of their climax. When Avra began to chuckle, Sam gave her a jerk.

"Quiet," he commanded.

"I'm just wondering if your head's clear."

Sam couldn't help joining in with the chuckling. "One is," he admitted.

They shared more laughter, before seriousness set in. The intensity of what was happening between them couldn't be kept at bay for long. Sam withdrew gingerly, tugging Avra off his softening sex. He kept her near for a hug.

Avra indulged, closing her eyes on the voice that whispered what they were doing was about more than sex. There was emotion cresting. She told herself it was just the drama of all that was occurring. She couldn't help but admit telling herself that enough times might eventually get her to believe it.

A grinding sound cut through the sound of the water rolling against the hull of the massive boat. The sound originated somewhere in the master cabin.

Sam recognized it and groaned. "'Scuse me, darlin'." He tapped her bottom.

Avra smiled, sliding down the stunning length of his body. "Tsk, tsk…so glad I forgot mine," she sang in reference to the vibrating cell phone. Sam slapped her bottom on his way past and she yelped.

He caught the phone midring, *midvibe,* and greeted his assistant, June Elliot.

"Now, this is what I like to hear. You actually sound happy." June's voice colored with laughter. "I take it you're glad you took the trip—sounds like the time away is doing you good."

"Hell, June, I've only been gone a day and a half."

"I know…that's why I don't relish making this call."

Sam worked his fingers along his nape. "I swear I can't take any more bad news, June."

"Oh, it's not that. At least…I haven't heard anything yet." She cleared her throat. "I did get a call from Libby Gerald, though."

"Yeah?" Sam recognized the name of his father's assistant.

"Mr. Dan has been trying to contact Detective Crest but it seems he's closed off the pipeline to the information he's been sharing."

"Maybe he's closin' in on a suspect," Sam reasoned, silently praying that suspect wasn't being given orders by his father or…anyone his father knew. He looked back at Avra then.

An Important Message from the Publisher

Dear Reader,

Because you've chosen to read one of our fine novels, I'd like to say "thank you"! And, as a special way to say thank you, I'm offering to send you two more Kimani™ Romance novels and two surprise gifts— absolutely FREE! These books will keep it real with true-to-life African American characters that turn up the heat and sizzle with passion.

Please enjoy the free books and gifts with our compliments...

Glenda Howard
For Kimani Press™

EDITOR'S
FREE GIFT
SEAL
THANK YOU

Peel off Seal and

Place Inside...

We'd like to send you two free books to introduce you to Kimani™ Romance books. These novels feature strong, sexy women, and African-American heroes that are charming, loving and true. Our authors fill each page with exceptional dialogue, exciting plot twists, and enough sizzling romance to keep you riveted until the very end!

KIMANI ROMANCE...LOVE'S ULTIMATE DESTINATION

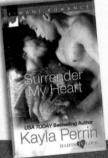

Your two books have a combined cover price of $12.50 in the U.S. or $14.50 in Canada, but are yours **FREE!**

We'll even send you two wonderful surprise gifts. You can't lose!

THE EDITOR'S "THANK YOU" FREE GIFTS INCLUDE:

➤ Two Kimani™ Romance Novels
➤ Two exciting surprise gifts

YES! I have placed my Editor's "thank you" Free Gifts seal in the space provided at right. Please send me 2 FREE Books, and my 2 FREE Mystery Gifts. I understand that I am under no obligation to purchase anything further, as explained on the back of this card.

PLACE
FREE GIFTS
SEAL
HERE

168/368 XDL FTF5

Please Print

FIRST NAME

LAST NAME

ADDRESS

APT.#   CITY

STATE/PROV.   ZIP/POSTAL CODE

Thank You!

The Reader Service - Here's How It Works:

Accepting your 2 free books and 2 free gifts (gifts valued at approximately $10.00) places you under no obligation to buy anything. You may keep the books and gifts and return the shipping statement marked "cancel." If you do not cancel, about a month later we'll send you 4 additional books and bill you just $4.94 each in the U.S. or $5.49 each in Canada. That is a savings of at least 21% off the cover price. Shipping and handling is just 50¢ per book in the U.S. and 75¢ per book in Canada.* You may cancel at any time, but if you choose to continue, every month we'll send you 4 more books, which you may either purchase at the discount price or return to us and cancel your subscription.
*Terms and prices subject to change without notice. Prices do not include applicable taxes. Sales tax applicable in N.Y. Canadian residents will be charged applicable taxes. Offer not valid in Quebec. All orders subject to credit approval. Credit or debit balances in a customer's account(s) may be offset by any other outstanding balance owed by or to the customer. Offer available while quantities last. Books received may not be as shown. Please allow 4 to 6 weeks for delivery.

If offer card is missing write to: The Reader Service, P.O. Box 1867, Buffalo, NY 14240-1867 or visit www.ReaderService.com

BUSINESS REPLY MAIL

FIRST-CLASS MAIL   PERMIT NO. 717   BUFFALO, NY

POSTAGE WILL BE PAID BY ADDRESSEE

THE READER SERVICE

PO BOX 1867

BUFFALO NY 14240-9952

NO POSTAGE
NECESSARY
IF MAILED
IN THE
UNITED STATES

"At any rate—" June sighed "—I called because there's been a holdup with the ad-crew folks at Ross."

Sam crossed an arm over his chest. "What kind of holdup?"

"They weren't specific but called to let you know they wouldn't be arriving this week for sure."

"Hell," Sam muttered a third time.

"Sorry, I could tell you were really relaxing down there."

"Right." Sam watched Avra venturing deeper into the bathroom for another shower.

"Well, I'm happy to hear it anyway, 'specially since you had to take the trip with Avra Ross. Oh! Her people asked me to get word to her about the schedule change. They've been trying her cell with no luck."

Sam's features hardened. "I'll let her know."

"So when can I expect you back?" June asked.

"Oh…" He bowed his head and smiled. "I may ditch a few more days. Can you make it that long without me?"

June laughed. "I can see your time away hasn't done a thing to tamp down that ego of yours."

"You take care, June. I'll see you soon," Sam said once the laughter softened between them.

After the call Sam hefted the slender mobile against his palm and debated. Steam rising from the bath snagged his attention and he dismissed his better intentions.

Later up on deck, Avra lounged. At least she *appeared* to be lounging while Sam grilled chicken for a late lunch. After their lengthy erotic session in the master cabin, followed by another round of showers,

Avra had brought the massive file to look through while Sam cooked.

"Nervous?" she teased, hearing the loud clatter of cookware followed by a hissed expletive.

"I don't get nervous." Sam's response was like stone.

"Oh, I believe you." She smirked and folded her bare legs beneath her on a deck chair. "I'm getting this is old hat for you. You should be a pro at this kind of stuff."

Taking interest in the statement, Sam stilled holding a long pair of tongs paused over the grill. "What *kind of stuff?*" he asked.

Avra's focus was on the file. "Entertaining women on your *Delilah*," she murmured.

There was another clatter followed by the shuffle of Sam's flip-flops as he left the grill. Avra looked up, surprised to find hardness shadowing his face when he stood before her.

"Sam—"

"Hush." He pointed at her with the hand that gripped a beer bottle. "What would you say if I told you Setha was the only woman who's ever been on this boat?"

Avra knew better than to continue the tease by telling him that no way in Hades was she buying that. Incredulously she stared up at him, also finding it hard to buy that her simple words had agitated him so.

"Would you believe me, Avra?"

"Yes, I— Yes, Sam."

"Right," he snorted, tilting the bottle to his mouth. He spared a quick, raking glare across her bare arms and legs courtesy of the scant nightdress she sported. Then he returned to the grill.

Avra shook her head and returned to the file. But

for the wind and soft waves bumping the boat, silence lingered between them…for a while.

"Sam!"

"Save it."

"Shut up and get your butt over here!"

He turned, tilting his head inquisitively when he noticed the set look on her face. He followed her order.

Avra grabbed his wrist and tugged him down roughly to look at the page lying open across her lap. Other than a worn topography map, Sam didn't find anything to shout *hooray* over. Unease mingled with his expression when he sent her a questioning look.

"Jeez…" Avra rolled her eyes and slammed her index finger downward in an exaggerated point.

Sam sighed but peered closer. His confusion cleared.

Chapter 10

"Where did you get this?" he asked. Sam hadn't looked up from the X-marked spot on the map since Avra pointed it out three minutes prior.

"Was in the stuff Setha gave me." She watched Sam, who had taken the map and sat studying it from the deck chair nearest her. "Came directly from Carson Arroyo."

"How'd *he* get it?"

"According to his mother, he's always been obsessed with knowing what had happened to his father."

Sam stretched out his legs and crossed them at the ankles. "When'd you see her?"

Avra twirled a wayward curl atop her head and thought. "Not long before Carson was shot, and I haven't talked to her since. But she did say that he took what happened very hard."

"Hard enough to dish out a little revenge?" Sam's tone was absent, his eyes fixed on the map.

It was a rhetorical question. Avra was sure that it was. "Isn't that obvious given all that's happened?" she replied anyway.

"All that's happened *happened* when we were kids. How the hell would he know how to put it all together? Where to start looking? Did his dad keep some kind of journal or something?"

"It's possible." Avra shrugged. "But if he did, what would've been in it?"

Sam fingered the whiskers roughening his jaw. "Probably whatever got him killed."

"Do we know who the money's goin' to?" were Brad Crest's words to his first lieutenant when they met to discuss what information had been uncovered.

"That's good, boss." Greg Roth's voice was hushed in obvious admiration.

Brad shrugged. "Makes sense. Viejo was killed— somebody had to benefit. Maybe the same somebody who was afraid he'd spill the beans about what's really goin' on here."

"You think he was blackmailing someone?"

"Nobody keeps this kind of info hangin' around less they intend on usin' it." Brad cast a venomous look toward the files and papers filling his desk.

Greg scratched at his receding hairline. "Maybe it was his insurance policy."

The thought intrigued Brad. "I'm listening." He reclined in the glossy black leather chair behind his desk.

"Well, it's obvious the guy ran with some big players. Maybe they were afraid he'd reveal some of this stuff if they got any ideas about layin' a hand on him."

Grimacing, Brad raked a hand through his blondish-brown locks and scanned the crime-scene photos of Martino Viejo. "Yeah, Greg, looks like someone got that very idea."

"Lieutenant." A young officer had knocked on Brad's door and then stepped in and left quickly after passing a file to Greg.

"Dammit," Greg breathed, grimacing at whatever the file contained.

"We found another set of journals," Greg began to explain to his boss. "They were full of all these names but there wasn't anything all that distinguishing about them until we got into Viejo's computer. We found the same lists there," he added when Brad's stare narrowed. "But in addition to the names, there were numbers, but there was still nothin' we could make any real sense of."

"Until?" Brad had a hunch there'd been a break. A serious one.

Greg handed his boss the file listing the names and numbers. He also passed him a card—on it was a single phrase and a number circled.

"Dammit." Brad repeated his lieutenant's earlier swear. "It's from the address."

"Check out the names, boss."

Nothing stood out initially. Brad drew a page closer, following what he read by the tip of his index finger. He stood with the list and went to the coffee table and shuffled through more papers. "Greg, this is a hit list."

Greg leaned forward in the chair he occupied before Brad's desk. "Boss, I sure hope not. There're well over two hundred names in these journals. That list you have just lists 'em from 09 to present. We've pulled lists from Viejo's computer goin' all the way back to the '70s."

Greg went on and removed the tie already loosened at his neck. "We're thinkin' that explains all the journals we found at his house. Probably held on to 'em after he was able to put all the data in a system."

"But data for what?" Brad grumbled, still focused on the printed lists. "Is there anything detailing more to link the folks on these lists?"

"Nothin' yet, boss."

Irritated, Brad kicked one of the coffee table's stout legs. "We're standin' here with one of the biggest damn pieces to the puzzle and can't put any of it to use."

"A road map sure would be helpful," Greg groaned.

Brad cocked a brow. "Ya think?"

"Damn thing's useless," Sam snapped and tossed the map to the low glass table between the deck chairs.

"Yeah, I guess…" Avra reached for the map and twisted her mouth. "Looks hand drawn. A kid could've done it."

Sam had gone back to the grill, where he worked in silence. Avra watched him situate sealed-foil vegetables to the rack for steaming.

"Sorry for making you handle all the kitchen duties."

"You're my guest." His voice had resumed its monotone.

"But we were forced to take this trip for business. It's not your job to pamper me."

"One good turn deserves another." He drove a long fork into the searing strips of chicken. "You've damn well been pampering *me*."

The soft acknowledgment held just enough suggestion to make Avra's cheeks burn.

Silence held on deck just a while longer before Sam broke into it. "Son of a— Avra? What was it you just said?"

"Huh? About being pampered?"

"Nah." He grimaced and went back to reach for the map. "Like this was drawn by a kid."

"Yeah…"

Sam paced with the map and scratched the top of his head as he concentrated. "You said this came out of Carson Arroyo's stuff. John Holloway was my dad's liaison down there for years. He was in charge of recruitment. He and his crew acted as go-betweens for MM and new employees." He'd stopped scratching the top of his head, but kept his hand there on the top. "The idea was to help 'em get settled in new positions. That's where he met his wife." Sam rubbed the muscles suddenly bunched at his neck. "They lived down there… hell…over ten years after the second son was born."

Avra had done a complete 180 in her deck chair to watch him pace. "Down where?" she asked.

"Mexico."

"You're a hard man to get on the phone, Detective Crest," Danilo was saying, palm outstretched for shaking when he met Brad in the middle of the ranch home office at Machine Melendez.

"Sorry, sir, the case has folks on edge. We're under a lot of pressure to close it, understandably."

Dan coughed, masking the pain of the gesture with a placid look that sized up Brad. "Is that why you decided to grace me with an in-person visit?"

"I've always looked up to you, sir. I owe my job to you."

"Cut it out, Bradley." Dan was clearly in no mood for having his ego stroked.

Brad took a turn at coughing then. "We're closin' in on whatever the hell this is, sir." His expression was then placid, as well. "We're gonna find out why those people were murdered—*your* people, *your* employees."

"What is it you want to know, Bradley?"

Brad eased both hands into the pockets of his pin-striped tan trousers. "Is there anything you want to tell me, sir? Before we uncover anything else?"

Dan's dark, heavy brows drew close over his deep-set eyes. "This a threat or a handout, Bradley?"

"It's a chance for you to salvage a reputation I believe's about to go down the toilet, *sir*."

"You little punk." Dan's outrage was interrupted by another cough attack. "How dare you…"

Brad raised his hands. "I didn't come here to be disrespectful, sir. But too many things are pointing an ugly finger at MM. If there's something you need to tell me—"

"Take your handout and *get* out."

Brad nodded, his blue gaze solemn. "Sir, I'm askin' you to think about this. Think about your kids, especially Setha. She's about to get married—a family scandal is the last thing any of you needs—"

"You ingrate!" The coughing spell had left Danilo's voice with a gravelly edge. "Get out!" he raged, knocking over a lamp in the process. More coughing resumed.

Brad turned to leave, barely nodding toward Libby Gerald when the woman rushed in to see to her boss. Brad heard her asking Dan whether he needed his pills. Regret over the loss of a longtime relationship cut deep but Brad wouldn't be swayed. He had a crime to solve.

* * *

Once the mystery of the map was no longer such a mystery, Samson and Avra delved into the notes with renewed interest. They were each exhilarated yet terrified over what they might find. They knew they couldn't turn back.

Unfortunately they were on leave for other matters, far removed from the solving of a mystery. Avra knew the crew would be arriving and their attention would be required for that, as well. When the fourth day aboard Sam's yacht appeared to be drawing to a close, she couldn't resist mentioning what had gnawed at her since the previous day.

She found Sam in the yacht's control room on a call with one of his pilots. Since the map discovery, he'd been trying to coordinate a trip. The fact that the address wasn't able to be located by GPS was putting a hitch in those plans.

"Any luck?" she called out from the entryway when Sam ended the call with a muffled curse.

He was knocking the black mobile against the wood-grained paneling of the counter space. "Would've helped if the kid knew coordinates when he made that damn map."

Avra smiled apologetically, hiding her fists in the hem of the melon-green T-shirt she wore with a pair of white shorts. "Does your pilot have any ideas?"

"I faxed him the map, but the quality's not the best. We're gonna meet back in Houston so he can take a look at the original." He swiveled the tall captain's chair around and studied her with a soft look. "Do you mind if I take it?"

"No." She shook her head quickly. "'Course not. Um…so have you heard whether the crew's checked in yet?"

Sam left the chair then. "Why?"

Avra's smile turned more daring. "I know the campaign's been a sore spot between us, but that *is* what we came down here for, remember?"

On bare feet, Sam padded slowly toward Avra, stopping when he stood right before her. "I know what we came down here for. But you do realize how important it is that we follow up on that?" He hitched a thumb over his shoulder in the general vicinity of the map.

"I know but—"

He wouldn't let her finish the thought. It required no effort for him to gather her scantily clad form against him. "How about we go into Kemah for dinner tonight?" He murmured the words into her skin as he nibbled her throat.

"Mmm-hmm…" The response was the best she could muster. Her heart thudded powerfully when he dragged her down with him to the floor. In a tangle of arms and legs they absorbed the friction stirring between their bodies.

Sam rose up and yanked the worn, wrinkled Dallas T-shirt over his head. "Maybe we'll make it for breakfast instead of dinner." His ego hummed at the sight of her grinding his thigh in need of his touch.

When he covered her, Avra was in heaven. She didn't care about playing the passive role and offered no resistance when he pulled her out of her shirt. Luxuriating in his touch, she rested her hands above her head and twisted her hips more provocatively. Softly, she uttered sighs of encouragement.

Sam needed no encouraging. He was already half-inside her shorts while his beautifully crafted and persuasive mouth hungrily worked on a nipple. The hand that skimmed her hip disappeared into the bottoms she wore with no panties.

He groaned over her nipple at the discovery and thrust three fingers into the hot, moist depths of her core. With his free hand he toyed with the nipple left bereft of his pleasure-providing lips.

At last Avra buried her hands in Sam's hair. She shivered at the sensation of his silk waves sliding between her fingers, caressing her palms. Samson was manipulating both her nipples then. His thumbs rubbed and flicked at the nubs while he inhaled the fragrant valley between her breasts. Gradually he eased down Avra's slender, curvy form. His body was insinuated between her thighs, forcing her legs apart to accommodate his size. She felt his fingers spreading the intimate folds of her sex and milliseconds later he was thrusting his tongue inside, rotating it sinfully as he did so.

"Sam…" His name was merely a breath passing her lips. She felt climactic less than a minute after he began to treat her but Sam wouldn't let up even when she pressed down on his shoulders.

"Inside me…" she demanded.

He took pity and moved to his feet in order to remove his denim shorts and boxers. He kicked them aside after taking a condom from the pocket and applying protection. Avra braced up on her elbows in an attempt to appreciate the full awesome view of him. It was a difficult move, but not impossible and sooo well worth the effort to observe every wide, muscular inch of his frame.

Sam offered her a hand up. Avra accepted, only to find herself perched on the edge of a desk in the control room. His broad endowment was filling her before her butt fully settled to the surface.

The big desk was swiped clear of everything it carried. The two enjoyed each other with a shameless rigor—each intent on outlasting the other. The muscles bunched and flexed along Sam's forearms as he held her leg across a shoulder and drove his erection home. Then, without breaking contact, he pulled her up, taking her with him to the tall captain's chair. He nibbled her ear while squeezing her bare bottom.

"I won't think less of you if you come before me," he growled into her breasts.

Avra's laughter was throaty. "Same here."

Sam tried laughing, but only managed a low grunt when Avra circled her hips in a new, naughtier manner. He squeezed her butt tighter, letting his head rest on the chair and giving himself over to the sensation she stirred inside him. Would he ever get enough of her? Only a few days and he didn't know how he'd resisted or accepted her resisting him for so long. Not wanting to think of it then, he captured her chin and kissed her deeply.

The act sent Avra into a frenzy. Hungrily, she worked to pull every ounce of her taste from his tongue. Her hips began to rotate in more lurid circles.

"I win…" she cooed, feeling him tense and then throb inside her as his release filled the condom.

In an enviable display of ease, Sam stood and took her with him. Kissing her jaw, he murmured, "Let's hear you bragging after round two."

Chapter 11

Setha knocked softly but rapidly against her father's room door that morning. Libby Gerald told her about his episode the afternoon before and the bad meeting with Brad Crest.

"Come." Dan's voice filtered through the tall walnut door.

The concern on Setha's lovely face gave way to mild agitation when she saw her father sitting up in bed. He held a paper and the laptop was on and waiting.

"Do you even have the slightest idea of what *rest* means?" she chastised.

Dan shook the paper. "I'll sleep when I'm dead."

The expression Dan put in place then had Setha's concern reasserting itself.

"Papa," she whispered, her sandaled feet shuffling tentatively toward the grand sleigh bed.

Danilo extended a hand, giving her silent leave to come to him.

"Why won't you talk to us?" she asked once curled tight against him.

"Ah, *bonita*." Dan chuckled, nuzzling his face into the dark, wavy mass of her hair. "I just let my anger get the better of me, that's all. All that anger and nothing to do with it. And since I couldn't hit a cop…"

Setha laughed. "So what Brad said was *that* bad?"

"Nothing for you to worry over, sweet." He rubbed her shoulders, visible thanks to the lavender sundress she wore.

"Dad—"

"You have better things to focus on. Like marrying my oldest friend's son. You don't know how pleased Basil and I are about this. Khouri's a good kid."

"We're *all* good kids, ones who worry when our fathers keep things from us. We're all adults now, Dad. Don't you think it's time to stop with the secrets?"

"Setha." Dan's tone held a warning tinge.

"Did Brad come to tell you about Shane Arroyo? Carson's brother?" Dan's expression gave Setha the answer she sought. "You haven't heard."

"I'm only halfway through the financial news." He gestured toward his copy of *Barron's*.

"He's dead, dad. Shot."

"You're sure?"

She nodded, settling back on her feet tucked beneath her rump. "Now, do you still want me to think there's nothing to worry about?"

Dan set aside the paper and took both Setha's hands in his. "Will you do your old man a favor?" He tapped an index finger to her mouth when she nodded. "Get yourself excited, overwhelmed and elated about getting married."

Setha blinked, feeling an unexpected rush of tears behind her eyes. Scooting close to Dan, she clutched the lapels of his nightshirt and hid her face in the crook of his neck.

"All right, Daddy," she murmured, "all right…"

As promised, Samson treated Avra to a fantastic breakfast. They docked in Kemah and took a leisurely stroll along the famed boardwalk to one of the area's popular restaurants. They were dining on platters of delicious fish and grits while noting how gorgeous the place was and sharing stories of childhood trips taken with their families.

"…those were the best trips when Mama was alive," Avra mused, failing to keep the somberness from her voice. "Just wasn't the same…after…"

Sam sought her foot under the table and nudged the toe of her sandal with his. "How did she pass?"

"In childbirth with my sister Fiona." Avra blinked and smiled ruefully. "It was hard suddenly being 'the woman of the house.' I wasn't ready for that at all…" She blinked again, realizing then how much she was sharing with him. "Sorry," she murmured and focused on chasing a lone shrimp around the edge of her nearly empty plate.

"Don't apologize." Sam's gravelly voice was quiet. He watched her for a bit and then studied their view from the restaurant balcony. "My mother grew up around here—just outside Galveston. That's where she met my dad—he worked one summer at her father's bait shop." Grinning then, Sam's dark gaze narrowed as it crinkled appealingly.

"My granddad wasn't about to let his only daughter

marry a Mexican—'specially one with no money." He joined in when Avra laughed, but sobered shortly after.

"My dad vowed to prove his worth and he did."

Warmth stoked a path along Avra's spine. She smiled over the beauty of the story. "Does your mom still have family here?"

"Everyone's pretty much scattered, but I keep a place on the land where my granddad had his shop."

"Another house?" Avra shook her head while leaning back on her chair. "You're quite the Realtor."

"It's not all that."

"Why don't I believe you?"

"We can head over after we finish up here. Spend the night."

Avra cast her expressive brown gaze upon the table and bit her lip, cursing herself when she did so. Dammit all, she thought. She'd never felt too uneasy around *any* man to voice her opinion no matter how unpopular it might be. She certainly never let a man bully her out of asking a question. She remembered the scene in the control room and wondered if she was letting Sam have that power now. Or was she deliberately stifling her questions because she knew she wouldn't like the answers?

Samson and Avra heard their names being called in the distance. They both recognized the two men who approached their table and they stood to greet them. Sam exchanged handshakes. Avra got hugs.

"What's goin' on, Harp?" Sam landed a friendly clap to Harper Sedgewick's back. The gesture was a bit heavier than necessary, but it was successful in getting Harp to release Avra, whom Sam felt he'd held on to for long enough.

The group stood on the sunny balcony conversing for a while. Harper Sedgewick and his partner, Edmund Covington, had been scouting new locales for their boating business.

"Y'all out enjoyin' the sights?" Ed asked.

"It's just business." Avra offered the explanation before Sam could speak up.

Harper and Ed merely nodded. Sam's expression harbored a noticeable edge.

"It was good seein' you guys." Avra wiped her hand across the seat of her jeans and reached for a tanned-leather canvas bag. "Would y'all mind keepin' Sam company for a bit? There's a store I want to check out—don't want to bore him to death while I window shop."

"Sure, Av!"

"No problem."

Sam shook his head minutely, observing the businessmen acting like two girl-crazy teenagers. Still, he wondered if any man could ever really say no to her. His guess was that those who did were very few and far between.

"I'll meet you back here in an hour, Sam, okay?" She was already retreating from the table.

"See you then." He smiled.

Silence lofted among all three men as they watched Avra leave.

"Very nice, man." Harper turned to apply a heavy clap to Sam's shoulder. "We wondered if you'd ever make that move."

Sam produced a black look and resumed his place at the table. "It's business, like she said."

"Right," Ed drawled, motioning for the server. "Kemah and business don't mix, partner."

"Toss in a sweetthang like Avra Ross—"

"And business is all it could be." Sam's stony tone was a perfect match to his expression.

Ed and Harper exchanged glances. They knew when it was time to stop teasing Sam Melendez.

"Hey, there!" the waitress greeted with a perky wave and twinkling blue eyes. "Can I bring you gentlemen some coffee while you decide on breakfast?"

Sam spoke for his associates. "Make it whiskey and you've got a deal."

Avra had been honing her business skills since the fourth grade. She'd learned to trust her instincts, and she always tried to listen to the well-meaning voices that warned her when something smelled like the inside of a spit can. This time all she wanted was to ignore her hunches and take Sam at face value. Lord knew he'd given her every reason to do so.

The days with him had been beyond spectacular and she never could have expected that. *Not* with Sam Melendez. Now here she was, going with her intuition, which would probably reveal things that would change her opinion of him and toss a wrench in whatever it was they may've had a shot at.

She stopped on the polished maplewood porch of the Brookings Tavern and Inn. The crew should have checked in the night before last. She was sure they'd try to contact her on the cell that was most likely sitting on the bed in her condo. She could've just as easily asked Sam if they'd tried calling him… She didn't want to admit that she believed he'd lie to her.

She gave a decisive tug to the tie on the cream wrap shirt she wore and ceased stalling. She went into the inn and headed for the front desk to wait patiently for the person to be helped in front of her. She was losing her nerve, when a second desk clerk arrived and smiled her way.

"Help you, ma'am?"

"I'm Avra Ross." She tried and failed to produce a decent smile. "Could you ring the room for the *Ross Review* ad teams?"

The clerk dutifully typed in the name on the computer and nodded when a new screen emerged. "Ah, yes," he said, "they haven't checked in, ma'am, but they did call…" He checked the old-fashioned letter holder behind the state-of-the-art desk. "Asked us to hold a message should you stop by."

"Thanks." Avra was already taking the folded note and flipping it open.

Rush job requires bulk of staff. Trip postponed one week—Khouri approved.

"Is there a phone I can dial out on?" She smiled when the clerk directed her to a burgundy phone at an end of the long desk.

"What the hell's goin' on? Why didn't y'all call me?" were Avra's first words when her assistant answered his phone line.

"Avra, calm down," Paul Tristam urged, not thrown the least bit off course by his boss. "We've been *trying* to call you since before the decision was made not to make the trip. Finally had to go to Khouri for approval to push it back a week. Why aren't you answering your phone? We left a ton of messages. We even called Sam Melendez to let him know."

Massaging her neck and the soreness she'd been trying to ignore, Avra closed her eyes. "That's what I was afraid of."

"What? Say again, Av. I didn't catch that."

Avra had spoken the whispered comment for her benefit only. "Thanks, Paul." She spoke louder that time. "I'll be home soon." She broke the connection and then pressed the receiver to her forehead.

After meeting up with Sam back at the restaurant, Avra maintained a mostly detached demeanor for the rest of the day. They'd returned to the yacht by early afternoon and Sam set course for West Bay, Texas.

Avra kept to her cabin for much of the trip. Sam didn't bother her, realizing he needed the distance, as well. It smarted to know it was business as usual with her despite all they'd done during the course of the trip.

It smarted even more to know he'd viewed their sexual endeavors as a possible start to something more. Meanwhile *she'd* viewed their interludes as a way to pass the time. He knew she had her reservations. She had reason to be skittish, considering the drama fest that had made up their association with one another. This time away was supposed to help them see past all the nonsense. It had sure as hell worked for him. Why hadn't it worked the same for her?

Because you knew what this trip was really about while she came thinking it was about business.

Sam muttered an expletive in reference to the simple truth. It was an insignificant portion to a larger matter, he told himself. Business or not, she should have been able to see that this was more than sex. There'd always been something more, even when they were at each other's throats.

The voice returned, telling him what he already knew. None of that mattered. He'd lied to her and, given all the previous negatives in their relationship, that *insignificant* portion was going to be hard for her to deal with. There would be hell to pay once she discovered it.

Samson's Delilah was docking outside the home Sam kept along the shores of West Bay, Texas. The place was hailed for its fishing and beckoned serious sportsmen, and women, in droves.

From her cabin Avra could sense the subtle shift in the boat speeds. She came up to take in the vessel's land approach. The house was, not surprisingly, an impressive sight. Obviously custom-built for Samson Melendez, the jackass, she thought and grudgingly admired the dwelling.

She grimaced at her anger. What he'd omitted was such a petty matter. *Probably an oversight,* she reasoned, resting her elbows along the railing as she considered it. She could have believed that if she didn't know Sam as well as she did. Regardless of how laid-back and cool he came off, his mind was always working. It was simply one of the reasons why he was the obvious choice to one day assume control of MM.

The yacht bumped to a stop once it reached the dock. Avra cast aside her thoughts and admitted she was curious to see whether the house was as impressive inside as it appeared from the pier.

"I'll start dinner as soon as I get our stuff from the boat!"

His rough, deep voice broke into her thoughts before she got too carried away over what she might find in the house. "Don't bother with dinner," she said, watching him sprint down the short stairwell leading down to the deck from the control room. "I've got a car coming," she told him, refusing to look away when he glared at her.

"What the hell is up *this* time, Av?"

Resting her back against the railing, she regarded him darkly. "I guess not much is up at all, Sam, since what we came down here for isn't going to happen. But then you knew that, didn't you?" She shrugged when he only plied her with a stony look. "Don't bother to lie. I got the truth when I went to check on the crew at the inn."

"Your window shopping?"

"Were you gonna tell me?"

"Would it have mattered, darlin'?" He was tall enough to lean back and rest his head against the stairwell's railing. "I get the feeling we'd be standin' here griping over one thing or another anyway. May as well have been this."

"After that big show you made about not signing the contract before the trip because *somebody* might pull somethin' shady?" Her voice was quiet but still accusing. "I guess you're the only one who gets to do that, huh?"

"What's this really about, Avra? You had your butt on your shoulders long before you went off to that inn."

"I didn't—"

"The hell you didn't." He came to crowd her against the railing, securing a hand on either side of her along it. "What was all that to Harp and Ed about us being here for business?"

"Because I thought we were."

"Bull." He took his time to study the way the wind whipped her curls above her dark face. "We haven't talked once about that campaign since we got here." His wide mouth curved briefly into a smile. "Maybe you're gonna tell me that's because I kept you on your back the whole time? Don't bother to lie." With those words he turned to walk away but stopped several feet later and tossed her the house key. He smiled when she easily caught it.

"Make yourself comfy." The hospitable words held little hospitality. "I'll have your stuff waiting by the time your car gets here."

Chapter 12

The following Friday evening Samson's ranch home was alive with the sounds of family and music. Lights sparkled all over the place as members of the wedding party mingled following the rehearsal. The clink of glasses and laughter followed boisterous toasts and had the crowd in high spirits.

The host even managed to have a fine time despite the fact that he'd been in a frightful mood for over a week. The news of Shane Arroyo's death had done even more to sour Sam's frame of mind. Then there were the meetings with his pilot. After reviewing the original map, which Avra had been kind enough to leave behind, there were no breakthroughs. No one had a clue as to how best to go about pinpointing a route to 14918 Figueroa Trail.

One hand settled in the pocket of tailored tree-bark-colored trousers, Samson leaned against one of the majestic columns lining the grand patio that almost spanned the length of the house. Drink in hand, which he'd mostly nursed, he observed the festivities from afar.

He and Avra had done a fine job of avoiding one another during the rehearsal and she'd made herself scarce afterward. His guess was that she'd tried to make a discreet exit. He'd noticed Khouri heading off after her and figured little brother had threatened bodily harm if she even *thought* about leaving.

The possibility made Sam smile. Before he grew too smug, however, his little sister walked up and slapped the back of his head.

"Dammit! Setha, what the hell—"

"What'd you do to Avra?" She glared, fists propped to hips, giving her the appearance of an avenging angel in the petal-pink dress that billowed about her legs. "We sent y'all there to have fun, not to make each other miserable as usual."

"Really?" Sam raised his brows to fake the appearance of innocence. "I thought we went down there for business."

"Cut the crap, Sam. What'd you do?"

"Why am *I* automatically the bad guy?"

Setha only folded her arms across the square bodice of her dress and waited. It didn't take long for Sam to break.

"You deserve more than a knock on the head," she said once he'd confessed.

"It was petty—even *you* have to admit that, Set. I can't believe she got so twisted over it."

"Need I remind you of the fool you made of yourself over signing the contract?"

Sam drained his glass, stubbornly refusing to acknowledge any wrongdoing. "And I signed the contract beforehand, didn't I?" He sounded like a little boy working doggedly to have the last word.

"But *she* doesn't know that, does she?" Setha watched him curiously when he groaned and set down the glass to rub his hands over his face. "What's going on with you? For real, Sam. You're not one to beat around bushes."

"It's different with her," he grumbled, voice muffled behind his hands before he moved them. "It's always been different with her."

"And why is that?"

"Setha." He began to stalk the porch. "Why are you torturing me with this?"

"'Cause it's so much fun."

"You're gonna make me say it, aren't you?"

"Uh-huh..."

He rolled his eyes while muttering a wicked curse. "She's it, all right?"

"Honey." Setha moved before her brother to halt his progress around the porch. "That scares you."

"Nothing scares me."

"Right."

"She's just so bullheaded." Sam made a strangling gesture with his hands. "So damn hard to talk to."

"Wow...she sounds like someone I know."

"I screwed up." He sighed again, leaning next to one of the porch columns and folding his arms across his chest. "I don't know how to make this right, Set."

Setha leaned against his arm and squeezed. "Sounds like she believes you don't think you did anything wrong and I'm sure she's got good reason to feel that way. Maybe you could try being honest with her?"

Sam rubbed at his eyes. "And if she tells me to go screw myself?"

Setha kissed his cheek. "Then I'm afraid you'll have to accept that and let her be angry for a while, but don't you dare give up."

"She's so damn tough, Set."

"Mmm…yep, just like someone I know."

Khouri was in the living room teasing his sister—quite thoroughly—over the fact that he'd never seen her run from a fight.

"I'm not fighting. I just want to go home." Avra smoothed her hands along her arms. The ankle-length emerald-and-navy dress was an empire-waisted number that bared her arms and accentuated her softly curved, willowy body.

Khouri spared a moment to pity his sister. He could detect the weariness in her voice. Whatever was going on between her and Sam Melendez was weighing heavy on her steely nerves. He knew without a second of doubt that she was in fact running and how much she'd hate herself for it later.

"You at least need to eat something," he said when she looked his way.

"I've got food at home."

Khouri's very light eyes sparkled as he laughed. "Yeah, all two cans of chicken-and-rice soup, a loaf of bread and tea."

Fire kindled in her vibrant coffee stare. "You know what, Khou? Forget you." She made a move to brush past him and was promptly stopped when he caught her upper arm.

"Damn you, Khouri." She bristled against his hold but suffered defeat when he relieved her of the car keys she gripped. "Why don't you go tend to your own relationship and leave mine alone?"

"Ah..." Khouri's sleek brows rose over his striking stare. "So there *is* a relationship between you and Sam?"

"Khouri, I swear..." Avra closed her eyes.

"Besides, my relationship is being tended to just fine. I'm getting married, remember?"

"Yeah...yes, you are." Avra couldn't help smiling. She was so very happy for her brother. Aside from her father, he was the most excellent man she knew. She'd never tell him that, of course.

"You *better* be getting married, else I'm takin' back that trip I bought y'all."

"Oh, no, that's way too good to be returned. We'll be keepin' that one, thank you very much."

Avra clasped her hands to her chest in a pleading gesture. "Couldn't you thank me by letting me go home?"

"Sure. After dinner."

"Jeez, Khouri!" She punched a pillow on her way past the sofa. "Brothers are supposed to defend their sisters against the creeps of the world, you know?"

"And if he were that, I would."

"Dammit, Khouri! I just told you what he did!"

"He's a guy, Av. Entitled to a few stupid moves here and there."

"Uh-huh, spoken like a stupid guy."

"Aw..." Khouri pulled her close for a hug. "What he

did was foul, but not as bad as it could've been. And if it makes any difference for you to know…he signed the contract right after you left the kitchen that morning."

Avra was jerking back to look her brother in the eye just as a knock fell on the door. Sam peeked inside.

"Y'all all right in here?" His eyes were fixed on Avra.

"Yep! We're good." Khouri kissed Avra's temple and then fingered her keys. "You'll get these back after dinner." On his way out of the room he clapped Sam's shoulder and pulled the door closed behind himself.

Samson moved deeper into the living room and Avra retreated.

"I'm walking you down the aisle." He smiled when she spun to face him, blinking and surprised by his words.

"Tomorrow for Set and Khouri's wedding." He shrugged, rubbing his hands one inside the other. "That won't be possible if you plan on avoiding me."

"Don't worry. I'll behave." She offered a lopsided smile. "I've been doing that all along, though, haven't I?"

One of the hands he rubbed clenched. "Hell, Avra, can't you get past that?"

"Exactly what am I getting past, Sam? That you lied to get me into bed or that you didn't tell me the crew's plans had changed? Both? Or is there something else you still haven't told me?"

"I'm sorry, Avra."

Her expression cleared. "Huh?" She was prepared for a fight—not an apology.

Sam massaged his neck while walking the space between the sofa and fireplace. "We slept together before I got that call about the crew. We slept together many times."

The soft element he could bring to his gravelly, deep voice made her shiver. Her cheeks burned despite the shiver and she pressed her hands against them—willing them to cool.

"When that call came through—all I could think was how I didn't want it to end. All I've known with you has been anger and squabbling, but this…" He closed his eyes and his sculpted mouth curved over the memory of it. "I never thought we could have that." Briefly he spread his hands. "I'm sorry—I was wrong not to tell you. I knew you'd think I did it just to get you into bed, but I did it to keep you there, which was just as bad."

Avra couldn't move or speak, for that matter. Sam stood rubbing his hands together and looking around the room as though he were uncomfortable in his own home.

"Well—" he clapped his hands once "—that's all I have. All I can say. I understand if you still think I'm full of crap, but I hope it's good enough for us to get along tomorrow for my sister and your brother." He graced her with a small smile and then left the room.

Avra gave in to the trembles that had threatened to surface since she heard his apology. She wanted to accept his words but she was supposed to hate him, wasn't she? They'd been at each other's throats since they'd met.

That didn't matter, though. Not now. Not when she'd fallen so deeply and intensely in love with him.

The wedding of Khouri Adande Ross and Setha Bianna Melendez was set for early evening the following Saturday. Guests arrived in their finest white linen and prepared for an exquisite evening of fun, romance and love.

Lanterns dotted the S. Melendez Ranch and basted the place in an ethereal glow. As the wedding was slated to be one of the biggest society soirees of the year, news helicopters jockeyed for airspace. Crews attempted to capture footage of A-list celebrities, star athletes and other elite members of the lengthy guest list before the scheduled blackout Sam had arranged to keep the rest of the event private. The media would be alerted once the bride and groom were pronounced husband and wife.

Avra decided to check in on her sister-in-law-to-be shortly after she arrived at the ranch. Judging from the slew of women, Raquel and Fiona included, stylists and makeup artists, Avra figured the girl was in good hands. As for herself, Avra also figured being in love hadn't made her any more interested in bridal festivities.

Besides, she had plans to spend time with another guest before the ceremony began. She strolled the grounds, waved dutifully but otherwise ignored the interested looks she drew. The toga-style cream satin gown she wore was a strapless frock that enhanced her backside and bustline while a minute train followed her.

She caught sight of her father talking as he stood amid a circle of men. It was her father she wanted to see. She wouldn't let herself get sidetracked with trying to scope out Samson. Her revelation the night before now had her more on edge than she'd ever been at any other time. Shaking away Sam's devastating image was impossible so she settled for pushing it away from the front of her mind.

"Well, I for one have better things to do!" Gaston Raines was a man who insisted on shouting to be heard despite the fact that his robust voice could be deafening even if he whispered. The man disengaged himself from the circle of his colleagues.

"Kissin' a mighty fine li'l thang is always a better way to spend time!" Gaston laughed while tugging Avra close when she approached the group.

"Hey, Mr. Raines." Avra accepted the kiss to the cheek and the hug Gaston requested next.

"All right, Gas, just you remember that's my baby girl!" Basil reminded his old friend and joined in when everyone else roared with laughter.

"Could I have a minute, Daddy?" Avra asked once she'd greeted the other three men in the circle.

"Gentlemen." Basil set his unfinished drink on the tray of a passing waiter and offered his daughter his arm.

"We were supposed to have a meeting this morning." Avra spoke through a tight smile.

"It's your brother's wedding day, miss." Basil's voice sounded sweet but held a firm undercurrent.

"I've been trying to meet with you every day for the past week. See anybody you recognize?" She held up a photo.

"Where did you get this?" Basil halted his steps, his eyes going right to the images of a young Luc Anton and Vita Arroyo in the top left of the picture.

"Such a coincidence. Why do you think Carson Arroyo would give Setha a picture like this? Even more of a coincidence is the fact that Carson and his brother are dead. Vita's husband is dead…" Avra slipped her hand from the crook of Basil's arm.

"Still not enough coincidence for you, Dad? I've got another picture of Luc Anton in front of this same building with Danilo Melendez—it was taken by you." She crossed her arms over the dress's ruched bodice. "If you can't quite place it, there's a nice replica covering an entire wall in Sam's den."

"I don't think I like your tone, young lady."

"And I don't like the fact that this whole thing stinks. You and Dan seem to be right in the middle of it." She stopped, seeing that her words had cut through her father's granite veneer. She took pity, slipping the photo back into her clutch bag and stepping closer to squeeze Basil's hands.

"Please, Daddy, talk to me or Khouri before there's another murder."

"Avra, do you think we—"

"No! No, Daddy, *I* don't think that, but if me and Setha were able to uncover this much, how long do you think it'll be before the police do the same?" She squeezed his hand a bit more insistently. "The most innocent things have ways of being twisted, Daddy. As a reporter you've seen that often enough, haven't you?"

Basil bowed his head. "Yes—" he sighed "—too often."

"Daddy—"

"No, love." Basil shook his head and turned tables to squeeze her hands then. His expression had taken on a reminiscent quality as he studied Avra's dark, oval face. "Dan and I weren't even as old as you are now when we began to make our fortunes. Most great fortunes have brutal beginnings…"

"Daddy...*talk* to me."

"Sweetie, this isn't just about me."

"Are you just afraid to reveal confidences or...is someone blackmailing you?" Her gaze turned stormy. "Is it Dan Melendez? Is that why *Ross Review* has written those fluff stories about MM all these years?"

Chimes rang out before Basil could either confirm or deny his daughter's suspicions. The melodic bells instructed guests to take their places—the ceremony was about to begin.

Avra caught Basil's arm when he turned away. "Dad—"

"It's your brother's day, miss."

Avra accepted that there would be no further discussion on the matter. She didn't attempt a smile when Basil cupped her cheeks and dropped a quick kiss to her forehead before he walked away.

Sam went to Avra when he saw her enter the hall where the bridal party was lining up for the procession. The closer he got, the easier it was for him to tell she wasn't herself.

"Hey?" He took her by the elbow and made her face him. "You all right?"

The simple inquiry broke down her walls. A shudder ripped through her as she covered her face with her hands.

Sam's hold on her elbow tightened and he pulled her off to a slightly less occupied corner of the hall. "What happened?" He dipped his head to peer closer into her eyes, his thumbs gently brushing at the tears clinging to her lashes.

"I've never seen my father afraid—many things, but never afraid."

"Honey—"

"I showed him the picture. The one with Lucas Anton and Vita Arroyo—he looked…like he'd seen a ghost. He got all weird, talking about how great fortunes having brutal origins and—and how it wasn't just about—about him."

"Honey, shh…" Sam squeezed her bare arms and shoulders. The panicky undertone of her voice singed his heart.

Avra savored the closeness when he tucked her into the side of his torso. She could feel him nuzzling his face into the top of her head. She curled her nails into the crisp fabric of his white tuxedo jacket and let it all drift away.

Her worry, concerns, fears all shimmered into utter contentment stemming from the simple act of his touch. Her eyelids felt heavy as if she were drowsy. His hands roaming her waist and back was more soothing than any massage. The sound of the wedding planner clapping and calling everyone to attention was an unwelcome but necessary intrusion.

"You ready to do this?" Sam murmured the words near her temple.

Avra soaked in a few more seconds of the closeness and then pushed back from his chest and nodded. She clutched the arm he offered and they took their places in line to await the start of the ceremony.

Chapter 13

The wedding was a breathtaking, intimate affair in spite of the enormous guest list. Several pairs of eyes grew teary in response to the heartfelt vows exchanged between the bride and groom. There was laughter when it appeared Setha's maid of honor had misplaced Khouri's ring and roaring applause when the couple was pronounced man and wife and then sprinted down the aisle as Mr. and Mrs. Khouri Ross.

Samson and Avra had kept close to each other since arriving arm in arm at the start of the affair. Sam knew it was worry over her father that kept Avra near. He wasn't going to complain. He had the feeling there would be more than a few society columns that would pick up on their closeness. He didn't care. Part of him, *a big part,* welcomed that. He knew she was his. It was time everyone else did, too.

And what of Avra? They hadn't discussed his apology or her acceptance—or denial—of it. Sam wasn't sure he wanted to know—not just then anyway. He was far too comfortable having her on his arm to concern himself with anything that might change that.

Chief Bradley Crest rarely got time off work. Chasing down leads in or around Houston was usually the only chance he had to see the city he called home. Thankfully, his wife, Cecily, was popular enough to score invites to the best events—case in point the Ross-Melendez wedding.

Brad had no intentions of denying his wife the outing or his presence there, as well. He knew one of his detectives would most likely wind up investigating *his* death if he had. Of course, duty could and always would find a way to intrude.

The all-too-familiar vibrating against his hip had Brad grimacing as he reached for the mobile he wore there. He wasn't surprised to find the name of his first lieutenant flashing on the screen. Swiveling his chair from the bar where he waited for drinks, he took the call.

"This better be good, Greg."

Gregory Roth chuckled. "Well, at least I waited till after the nuptials."

"How did you know—"

"Well, everybody at the precinct's got a TV turned to one of the news channels. They're always the first to announce these society marriages once the bride and groom tie the knot."

"Greg, I'm impressed." Brad chuckled. "Didn't know you were such an entertainment-news buff."

"Funny…so, you got a sec?"

"Am I going to like this?" Brad nodded toward the bartender, who had set down the drinks he'd ordered.

"You'll like it better if you can make sense of it."

Brad passed the bartender a generous tip. "Shoot," he said to Greg.

"The info from those discs all contained copies of disclosure agreements signed by hundreds of new employees. Immigrant employees."

"Anyone we know?"

"At least five."

"Damn."

Brad rubbed sudden tension from his forehead. "So what are the agreements for?"

"That's what I'm hoping you can make sense of." Rustling carried over the line then as if Greg were shuffling papers. "There are no details. Whatever it's about is simply referred to as 'The Matter.'"

"Crap." Brad moved the rubbing to the nape of his neck. "Can this thing get any more convoluted?"

"This case? Nah…" Greg chuckled but was not amused. "Whatever 'The Matter' is, it was heavy enough to threaten these folks with being sent back home if they breathed a word about it. Boss?" Greg queried when silence held the line for more than a few seconds.

"Yeah?"

"What's our next move?"

"Keep diggin'." Brad sighed, looking out over the sea of well-dressed guests filling the east side of the ranch. "Turn over whatever rocks you need to."

"Okay…" Greg waited a moment. "We've, um… we've put names to most of the faces in Martino Viejo's photos. Given who those *faces* are we've held off on our questions till we have more to go on."

"Time for playin' the respect game is long past, Greg." Brad's voice was like stone. "You do whatever it takes to find out what this *'matter'* is. We get that and we've got our motive."

The newlyweds had already ventured upstairs to change clothes. They were to head off for their honeymoon shortly, but the reception was scheduled to carry on into the predawn hours.

Avra had let Sam bully her into a dance when the music slowed. She hadn't seen her father since before the wedding and feared she'd go seek him out again if Sam hadn't been there to keep her occupied.

Pleasantly occupied, she thought while they swayed to a seductive Jill Scott piece. At least they'd *started* with swaying. Just then they were merely hanging on to one another, barely moving to the melody.

"Seen two familiar faces from the local news," Avra noted in a lazy tone.

"And?" Sam murmured, his forehead resting comfortably on her shoulder.

"People will talk."

"People are already talking—wondering who the next couple will be to take the vows after Khouri and Set."

"Everybody knows we hate each other."

"Makes the story that much more exciting if it's us, then."

Avra moaned, causing Sam to lift his head. "That'd be some story." She smiled up at him.

His ebony gaze narrowed playfully. "Yes, it would." He cupped her face and dipped his head to kiss her.

"Sam." Avra bristled so slightly it might've been imagined.

His head fell back to her shoulder. "How long will you punish me for what I did?"

"I'm not punishing you."

Again, Sam raised his head. "Guess that means you're staying the night with me." He smiled when she broke eye contact. "Right," he muttered.

"Sam…" She pulled slight laughter into her voice. "You know as well as I do that we aren't cut out to be a couple. We'd just wind up making fools of ourselves—"

"Stop." His tone brooked no argument. He released her and left her alone on the floor as the music continued.

"Greg, my wife's getting suspicious." Brad chuckled when he took another call from his first lieutenant. "You're gonna have to stop callin' like this."

"Boss, we got somethin'."

"About the vics."

"In a manner of speaking. We pulled another file off one of the discs."

"Another disclosure statement?"

"It's a report—a police report."

Brad glanced across his shoulder while moving to a deserted section of the patio. "Police report."

"Regarding John Holloway's death."

"Holloway? Greg—"

"According to this report, Holloway was shot."

"Greg, we already know he—"

"Twice. In the temple and in the back of the head.

I'm thinkin' the one in the back of the head wasn't self-inflicted."

"Hell…" Brad leaned against the vine-covered trellis and brought a hand to his mouth. "How could Holloway's death be deemed a suicide with a report stating it was otherwise?"

"We only found this on Viejo's disc. There's no record of it in our database."

"What aren't you telling me, Greg?"

"You should get back here, boss."

"Greg—"

"You aren't gonna want to hear this over the phone, boss. Trust me."

Laughter was still running at full blast after Setha tossed the bouquet, which was caught by Dan's assistant, Libby Gerald. As the woman had never married, and had publicly stated that she had no fascination with the institution, speculation ran high as to whether or not superstition would turn into fact.

While Khouri was off somewhere speaking to his father, Setha sought out hers. She found him alone in the sunroom tucked away down a back corridor in an area of the house that had been off-limits during the wedding. Danilo was dozing on an overstuffed, oversize gray chair.

"Daddy?" Setha stood half in, half out of the room debating on whether or not to stay.

Without opening his eyes, Dan smiled and extended a hand toward his daughter. Setha ran to him, dropped into his lap and hugged him tight.

"You've made me a very proud man this day,

bonita." He kissed her mouth and then cupped her chin. "Be happy."

Setha's dark eyes sparkled with unshed tears of bliss. "I don't think I'll have any problem doing that, Daddy." Still, the delight on her face showed traces of unease about the edges. "Daddy—"

"Shh…" Dan angled his index finger across her lips. "These are joyful times and I'll see you enjoy every bit of them. I love you, *bonita.*"

"I love you, Daddy," Setha whispered and drew him into another hug.

Avra had made herself scarce during the throwing of the bridal bouquet. Lining up for that was the absolute last thing she wanted.

She left one of the upstairs washrooms and immediately scrapped that last remark. Lining up for the bouquet wasn't the absolute *last* thing. Getting caught upstairs alone with Samson Melendez had to be.

"Guess I'll be going" were the first words that came to her mind when she left the washroom and saw him leaning against the opposite wall of the corridor.

Sam offered no response and merely maintained his casual stance against the wall. Despite the hands in his trouser pockets, *casual* was the last thing he appeared.

Avra kept her head high, praying he'd let her pass. He blocked her way.

He blocked her entire view of the opposite end of the hall, for that matter.

"Sam, don't—"

"Stay." He advanced.

Avra retreated. "It's not a good idea."

"We're a very good idea. Why are you afraid of that?"

"I'm not afraid of a damn thing." Inwardly she grimaced at the prissy tone of her voice. "Why are you doing this, Sam? Going after a woman who hates your guts, when you can have anybody?"

"I don't think you hate me nearly as much as you keep trying to make yourself believe."

"Good night, Sam." She made a play at brushing past him, lips thinning when he took her up.

Things happened swiftly then. He had her against the corridor wall, his divine mouth slanting over hers. Avra gave in to the kiss without hesitation or question. She was moaning and twisting desperately against him so she barely noticed when he carried her down the hall and into a room at the end.

Richer sounding moans drifted past Avra's lips at the feel of plush firmness beneath her back. Languidly she snuggled into the bed he'd placed her onto.

"Nice dress." Sam spoke into her neck while his powerful hands skimmed the whisper-soft fabric and her body beneath it. "So easy for me to get into," he commended upon freeing one breast from the bodice. Hungrily, he suckled and licked. Sounds radiated from the depths of his throat while he unhooked the rest of the garment's fastenings.

She chanted for him to wait even as she worked at his shirt buttons.

Sam began working his way down her torso. His hands were beneath the dress, already pushed up over her thighs. Avra felt as though she were tumbling into a welcoming abyss and eager to let it swallow her. Somehow, and she had no earthly idea how, she resisted.

Taking advantage of the brief moment of clarity, she pressed at his massive shoulders. "Sam, I can't." It was true, wasn't it? Somehow she would manage to screw this up, whatever *this* was. "Sam, stop." She stilled in his arms.

The context of her words probed the edges of his conscience with greater force. Sam's sensual attention began to cool and he gradually took note of what she was telling him. He eased off but didn't completely move off her. He kept quiet but didn't need to speak in order to relay his mood. He pulled one hand through his hair and his lashes fluttered against the frustration claiming him. The gesture said more than enough about his state of mind. His obsidian gaze locked on her breasts he'd bared and hunger returned to mingle with frustration.

Avra saw it clearly and tugged at the front of her dress. "I'm sorry, Sam." She edged out from beneath him.

Sam dropped an arm across her waist before she could clear the bed. "Don't go." His handsome face nuzzled the side of her neck. "You don't want to go." His hand trailed another deliberate path beneath the dress, heading for the plush line of her thighs. Soon his fingers were grazing the crotch of her panties and then slipping inside to stroke her sex. They slipped into a creamy well of need shortly after.

The thrusts and rotations inside her body had Avra parting her lips and melting back onto the bed. Shamelessly she arched her hips to indulge in every stroke. She closed her hand over Sam's wrist, and he deepened the penetration, if that were possible. Avra bit her lip so hard she threatened to break the skin.

"Stay with me." His lips were fastened to her diamond-studded earlobe.

Her hold on his wrist tightened again and again as she used some superhuman exertion of will to resist. She gave an unexpected tug to his wrist, withdrawing him from her body and sliding from the bed quicker that time.

"I'm sorry, Sam." Her voice was faint. "I'm sorry." The words carried over her shoulder as she rushed from the room.

Chapter 14

The newlyweds had set off for their honeymoon around 9:00 p.m. on their wedding night. Speculation ran high regarding their destination, but understandably, lips were sealed tight on that entertaining tidbit.

Avra had taken over Khouri's workload in addition to her own. She assumed much of her father's responsibilities, as well. The latter had been unexpected, but not that much of a surprise. After their run-in before the wedding, Basil kept close to his home.

Avra regretted the tension she'd been at fault for placing in the midst of her and her father when they were usually so close. Unfortunately the issue at hand wasn't one that could be swept under the rug and forgotten. Quite obviously *that* had gone on long enough.

Losing interest in the requisitions she'd been studying, Avra pushed away the sheets and stood behind her desk. She threw her attention toward the windows and hoped a good long stare at her view would improve her mood.

She doubted she'd have much luck with that. She'd been agitated—*understandably* after the wedding. Since what took place after the wedding, she specified, hugging herself beneath the long-sleeved lavender body shirt. She hadn't seen nor spoken with Sam since then. The Ross ad crew was on its way to begin shooting for the new campaign. Neither her nor Sam's input was needed at that point.

Groaning softly, Avra planted her bottom on the edge of her desk. She'd forbid herself to even think of what had gone on between them. It had worked…for a while—a short while.

She couldn't get him off her mind. Where once the mere thought of him inspired the fiercest agitations, thinking of him now only made her realize how deeply she'd fallen for him.

"Nice, Avra…" She groaned again, hiding her face in her hands.

Police Commissioner Russell Otis's boisterous laughter threatened to shake the pictures and plaques right from the walls in his downtown office. He pushed back from his gargantuan desk, coming to his feet to meet Brad Crest in the middle of the room.

"Good to see ya, son!" Otis's voice still carried on laughter as he enveloped one of Brad's hands in a beefy grip.

"Good to see you, too, sir. Sorry for interrupting without an appointment."

"Aw." Russell Otis waved off the apology. "This is a good surprise. What can I do for you?"

"Sir, you know I'm working on the Melendez murders?" Brad's words hung on the question and he watched Otis nod.

"Awful crimes." Otis scratched at the few strands of gray hair combed over the crown of his head. "I've assured the mayor and city council that we'll bring the culprit to justice." His blue gaze narrowed. "Is that what you've come to tell me, son? You've caught the SOB responsible?"

"No, sir. Unfortunately, no." Brad's voice was riddled with weariness.

"Is there anything your people need? More man power, overtime hours?"

"Thank you, sir, but no, I'm not here for that."

"All right." Russell Otis folded his arms over his protruding belly and leaned on the edge of his desk. "Guess I'll just shut the hell up so you can get to the point."

"This case has so many twists and turns, sir." Brad tugged at the woven rust-colored tie that was suddenly too tight at his neck. "That's why it's takin' so long to solve this damn thing. We've uncovered a lot of leads but none of them started to connect until lately."

Otis nodded. "Three-quarters of police work is connecting a lot of little dots."

Brad reciprocated with a nod of his own. "And another part of it is deciding whether certain dots are a part of the picture or not."

"Humph, yes, indeedy, we do uncover a lot of useless info, don't we?"

"Yes, sir…but sometimes useless info is too incredible to be ignored."

Otis tilted his big head at a suspicious angle. "Why do I feel like we're talkin' in circles, son?"

"'Cause we are, sir." Brad turned to face his superior more directly. "Sir, what do you recall about the John Holloway suicide?"

The expectant look faded from Otis's face. In its place understanding settled in. Otis pushed off the desk and went to stand behind it, muscles bunched beneath the wrinkled beige fabric of his shirt.

"The man worked for Melendez…lost his job and couldn't handle it. Killed himself. Left behind a wife and two kids," he remembered.

"Sons," Brad clarified. "Carson, the youngest, was stalking Setha Melendez. The older one, Shane, was killed earlier last week. Carson's dead, as well—shot when he made another play for Setha."

Otis listened without reaction.

"We've worked hard to keep certain aspects of the case from the press and members of the force not directly involved in the investigation."

"You've done a good job." Otis's laughter was half-hearted. "I haven't heard a peep."

Brad winced. "With all due respect, sir, I find that hard to believe since Carson and Shane are Holloway's sons. That, plus the fact that the man didn't commit suicide as stated. He died from gunshot wounds, one of which he couldn't possibly have inflicted on himself. Sir, I find it hard to believe you haven't heard a *peep* since the Holloway case was yours and since you changed your report. You omitted info regarding the second gunshot wound."

Otis's *understanding* harbored traces of anger then. "I think you should stand down, Detective."

"I can't do that, sir. Not when I've got a growing list of murder victims."

"What's that got to do with this?"

"A copy of the original police report was found among Martino Viejo's things along with a fax cover sheet—recipient Carson Arroyo."

Otis seemed to lose strength to stand. He groped for the edge of the desk and leaned against it again.

"We know Arroyo's responsible for at least two of the murders." Brad shoved both hands into his trouser pockets.

"Why?" Otis's voice sounded faint.

"That's what I'm hoping you can tell me, sir. So we can solve this thing. What beef would Arroyo have had with Melendez employees other than the fact that they *were* MM employees? Was it a revenge thing against Melendez for firing his father? Is that why he went after Setha?"

"Oh…" Otis buried his face in his red hands.

"Sir, I need you to talk to—"

"No, Brad."

"Sir, we're extremely close to solving this thing."

Otis smiled wearily. "You don't have to warn me, son. I know the consequences of not cooperating in an investigation."

"I'm sorry, sir."

Brad stood close enough for Otis to clap his shoulder. "Don't apologize for being a good cop. A good cop is worth his weight in gold. Do you know why, son?"

"Why, sir?"

"Because they're rare."

Samson didn't immediately make his presence known when he arrived at *Ross Review* that afternoon.

He'd been surprised by the call that the ad crew had preliminary proofs of the campaign ready for viewing.

The surprise gave way to relief over the fact that he wouldn't have to rack his brain to think of a reason to see her. He missed her—missed her in the most basic way, yes, but dammit, he even missed their bickering.

He smirked, watching Avra from the doorway of the conference room where they were to view the presentation. She leaned against the long rectangular table that occupied most of the room and talked with people whom Sam assumed were members of her crew. He couldn't help grinning at the sound of her voice as she relayed comments that had her colleagues chuckling.

One of the men near the table noticed Sam in the doorway and nodded. Avra's smile dimmed just slightly when she saw him. The men made themselves scarce— all they could do since Avra had completely dismissed them the moment her eyes landed on Sam.

She watched him walk into the room. Emotion suddenly lodged in her throat and she had to clear her throat around it.

"Thanks for coming," she said.

He followed the path his index finger trailed on the table. "Is there some reason you thought I wouldn't?"

Avra opened her mouth to reply but couldn't.

"I'm sorry for all this…new tension, Av."

His words deepened her smile. "All these years I've known you, I've never heard you apologize more than you have in the past few weeks."

"I'm not tryin' to make a habit of it, trust me." A playful grimace softened the striking contours of his copper-toned face. "Guess you'd really be surprised if I told you I even miss our arguing."

Avra threw back her head and laughed. "We certainly talked more then—were probably more honest about things then."

Sam settled next to her on the edge of the table and nudged her slender shoulder with his large one. "Honest about what things?"

Shivers stirred gooseflesh beneath the flaring sleeves of her raspberry silk blouse. Other meeting attendees were arriving and she stifled her words reluctantly.

"Will you talk to me about it over dinner?" He leaned close to speak near her ear.

Avra studied her fingers. "I don't know if you're ready to hear it." Her voice was quiet.

Sam bowed his head. "Are you ready to say it?" His voice was just as quiet.

She looked at him then, and her coffee-brown stare appeared lost—bewildered.

He squeezed her chin. "I'll pick you up at seven."

Dan was on the way out of his ranch office that afternoon but stopped off to leave some papers for his assistant. At her desk Dan caught sight of one of the many pictures Libby Gerald kept of his kids. The photos of them, throughout the years, littered her desk, windowsill and file cabinets.

Given the fact that Libby had never married nor had children of her own, she more than made up for it by the motherlike concern she showed for Dan's group.

Perching on the edge, he took a look at the latest picture to dot the woman's desk. It was a photo of the newlyweds; Dan traced Setha's beautiful laughing face upturned toward her husband. He nodded, satisfied by the happiness and love radiating from the two young people.

If only he could get his three sons on that proper track. Dan chuckled over the fact. It would be easier to wrestle a family of Angus bulls than to interest those three in the institution of marriage.

"Don't even think about taking my photos!" Libby pointed a finger toward her boss when she walked through the door.

"I don't think you have room for any more on this desk, Lib." Dan grinned.

"Don't you worry about that. I've got plenty of room and a special place cleared for those grandbabies."

Dan's laughter filled the office. "And I thought *I* was bad!" He set down the photo and stood. "I left those papers that you needed."

"Great! I'll get 'em to accounting before I head home. You have a good night!" she called, seeing him on his way to the door.

"You, too." Dan was checking his trousers and suit-coat pockets for keys when the phone rang.

"Dan Melendez's office." Libby's pert, robust voice greeted the caller.

Dan paused at the door.

"Well, hi! How are you?" Libby placed a hand over the phone's mouthpiece. "Russell Otis," she said.

Dan chuckled and reached for the phone. "Russ!"

The good vibes lasted only a moment. Dan's expression dimmed and he began to work his fingers at his throat in a sign of obvious discomfort.

"Hold on," he told the police commissioner. "Send this to my office phone," he told Libby.

"Everything all right?" Libby's question was answered by silence.

"I refuse to make another move till you tell me what the devil has lit a fire beneath your behind." June Elliott had never seen her boss in such a hurry to clear his desk.

"Somethin' wrong with me turnin' over a new leaf, June?" Samson asked.

"I'll lean toward yes since I've never seen you do it before."

"Aw, Ju-Ju." Sam walked by and dropped a kiss to the woman's forehead.

"All right, I demand to know what's going on."

Sam paused from riffling through the files on his desk. "I've got a date."

"What else is new?" June stood unimpressed. "She must be something else."

"She's Avra Ross."

June whistled and leaned over to brace her hands on the edge of the desk. "No wonder you're tryin' to get right. Makes sense if it's to be your last night among the livin'."

Sam chuckled and resumed searching the files. "I don't expect any bloodshed."

"You're really excited by this?" June propped a hand to a generous hip and observed Sam curiously.

"It's scary." He shrugged. "I, um, I don't know if I've ever felt…" He shook his head as if uncertain about speaking the words.

"Happier?" June supplied.

Sam's smile was response enough.

"Well, then." June resumed her work. "So where are you taking her?"

"This new steak house downtown. Supposedly, they specialize in steak dishes from all over the world."

"Oh, yeah…I think the chef was on one of those food shows."

The phone rang amid the discussion and June leaned over the desk to answer.

"Hey, Lib! Mmm-hmm…well, sure—sure, honey, hold on. He's right here." She pressed the receiver to her chest. "It's Libby Gerald." She passed the phone to Sam.

"Hey, Miss Lib." Sam's deep voice was soft with sweetness. He listened patiently from the edge of the desk while going through the files in hand. Eventually his flips through the folders became slower. Then they slipped right from his fingers.

"He what? No, Miss Libby, I—" He shook his head, his voice growing softer with every word he uttered. "That can't be. I just saw him." His voice trembled.

June was waiting, watching with a mix of unease and expectancy lurking in her eyes. "Everything okay?" She looked on as he set down the receiver without replacing it on the cradle. "Sam? Sam!" she cried when he moved to take a seat and almost missed the chair behind his desk.

"Sam?" She patted his cheeks. "Honey, what is it? Sam, talk to me. What'd Libby want?"

"June." Sam rubbed a shaking hand across his brow. "Call my brothers."

Chapter 15

Emts were seconds away from reaching Danilo Melendez. Unfortunately it was too late. By the time they'd gotten to the office at Machine Melendez, the man had died from what had all the earmarks of a heart attack.

The ranch home office looked as if it was enveloped in a cloud of smoke. In reality it was dust from the tires of the many vehicles that sped down the dirt road toward the house.

Libby Gerald was seated on the porch among uniformed and plainclothes officers. She was delicately clutching a handkerchief and dabbing at her eyes as tears trailed down her cheeks in a profuse stream. She saw Sam and ran to him, her tears multiplying.

"We were laughing over all the pictures. He was so happy about Setha and we joked," Libby gasped, torn between elating memories and despairing reality. "We were talking about pictures of her babies…when she has them. Oh, Sam…" She dissolved into sobs.

Sam's eyes were red from his own share of crying. He could barely pat Libby's shoulders as she cried on his chest.

"Then he got that call…"

Sam eased back. "Did that upset him, Miss Lib?"

"I don't see why it would." Libby dabbed her eyes with the handkerchief. "Russ Otis is one of his oldest friends."

Brad emerged from the circle of officers. "Ms. Gerald, let's get you inside where it's cooler." He nodded toward one of the uniformed officers. "Get her somethin' to drink." He turned to Sam then and extended a hand.

"I'm sorry, man."

"Was it really a heart attack, B?" Sam asked when they pulled out of a brief embrace.

Brad nodded. "Looks to be. No foul play." He knew what Sam was really asking. "Do you know what Commissioner Otis may've wanted to talk to your father about?"

"No." Despite Sam's fresh grief, the question aroused his suspicions. "Do *you* know?"

Brad nodded to his officers and directed them to disperse. He pulled Sam to the far end of the porch and told him he suspected Russell Otis may have known something about the murders.

"Should you be tellin' me this, B?" Sam's shoulders appeared broader in the wake of his despair and tension.

"I want to solve this thing too much to worry over where I get my information," Brad said.

Sam had already lost interest in the conversation. His emotions rose once more like a storm and the wound it opened was raw.

Brad was still going on when he took note of Sam's cold expression.

"Sam?"

"I don't give a damn how you solve this case, so why don't you just save whatever information you decide to hand out."

"Sam—" Brad's tone reflected regret. "It wasn't my intention to upset you. You don't need that right now."

Sam worked his fingers over the bridge of his nose. He willed the tears behind his eyes not to show themselves.

Brad clapped Sam's shoulder and was about to walk away.

"Brad?" Sam kept his eyes closed and still massaged his nose. "Why are you so interested in that? What Commissioner Otis called my dad for?" He looked up when Brad hesitated with the answer.

"Please, Brad." Sam closed his eyes resignedly. "I can't go in there yet." He cast a dark sidelong glance toward the ranch-house door. "I can't go in there and deal with my brothers crying."

Brad nodded and squeezed Sam's arm reassuringly. "According to Ms. Gerald, your father got that call from Commissioner Otis little over ten minutes after I left Otis's office."

"So?"

"So I had just finished asking the commissioner why he falsified a police report proving John Holloway didn't commit suicide."

Sam blinked. "What?"

"That's what I was hoping Otis could tell me."

"How did you find this out?"

"The original report was in Martino Viejo's stuff. We found it along with a fax cover sheet—he'd sent it to Carson Arroyo."

Sam leaned against the siding. "And you think that's why the commissioner called dad?"

"I do." Brad's grim smile matched the look in his eyes. "Whatever this is about, I think it upset your dad enough to throw him into that heart attack."

Sam didn't need Brad to endorse that fact. He believed it was all too true. Commissioner Russell Otis was definitely in on the big secret if his being part of the group picture Sam's mural depicted was any clue.

Avra hadn't heard from Sam and doubted she would anytime soon. Their date had fallen through, of course. News of Danilo Melendez's death had rocked Houston. Regardless of social standing, Dan's death had touched everyone equally.

News broadcasts were already speculating whether the Melendez murders had reached an end with Danilo's death. This in spite of the fact that a heart attack was the cause of death. Clearly, the events of the past few months had taken their toll on the renowned entrepreneur.

It all put things into perspective for Avra. She didn't want to be at odds with her father no matter what he may have been hiding. Knocking lightly on the den door, she listened for his voice. Hearing nothing, she knocked again and then twisted the knob.

Given the time of evening, no light burning in the room left it in almost pitch blackness. From the hall lamps she could just make out her father's profile from where he sat in one of the armchairs facing the huge rear lawn of the house. Avra said nothing, only sat at Basil's feet and rested her head on his knee.

"Dan was the only one who understood what it was like to lose the love of your life." Basil's voice drifted into the room on a quiet wave. "We'd lost track of each other for a long time… Losing our wives changed that and we—we could meet on that level, draw strength from one another because of it…"

"I know, Daddy." She kissed his knee.

"I don't want to say goodbye to him, miss."

"But you know that you have to."

"I don't want to walk through a death house," he confided with a shudder.

"Daddy…" Avra hugged him tighter, knowing he was referring to the funeral home that had Danilo's body for viewing. She understood his reluctance. Basil had refused to attend another funeral following her mother's death. "You won't be alone, Daddy." She spoke into his pant leg. "I promise."

The viewing was held the next evening. Avra kept a tight hold on her father's arm from the time she helped him from the car until she'd escorted him into the funeral parlor. She relaxed her grip a bit then but clutched him again when they approached the casket.

Avra heard her father's sharp intake of breath when he looked down into the lifeless face of his best friend. She kept hold of his shoulders as he shuddered and gasped. She looked upon Sam with grateful eyes when he approached and pulled her father close.

"You two sit with me," he said.

One of the attendees took Basil to a seat. Sam pulled Avra just out of the main room to a quiet corner in the corridor. For a time he squeezed and held her hands, studying them as if they held him mesmerized.

"Sorry about our date."

"Shh." She pulled his hands up, pressing kisses to the backs of them. "I'm so sorry, Sam. You dad was a great man."

"My father was a great man with great secrets." His face was as hard as his voice.

Avra smoothed the back of her hand across his cheek. "Honey, don't do this. It's not the place—"

"It's exactly the place." Crowding her easily, Sam made quick work of sharing what he'd learned of the police report and Russell Otis's call to Danilo.

"Sam, calm down." Avra saw more people entering the parlor. "Let's go over this another time."

"When can I see you?"

"Anytime." She didn't hesitate. "But, honey, you need to focus on your family right now."

He nodded, squeezing his eyes shut as though he finally heard her—as though he finally agreed. "What about Khouri and Setha?"

"I talked to Khouri." She patted the handkerchief peeking out of the breast pocket of his dark suit. "They'll be here in time for the funeral."

The word broke into Sam's iron facade. Avra caught him as he crumpled. Whispering soothing words, she kissed his cheek and rocked him slow.

Danilo Melendez's funeral was no less of an affair than his wake had been. The funeral directors believed the number of attendees would far exceed the capacity of the parlor so a graveside service was put in place.

Tears, low humming and crying intermingled with the minister's eulogy. The threatening rain remained at bay but the heavy clouds stifled the sun. Mother Nature's concession kept the air cooler than it would have otherwise been for the early-afternoon service. For the second time in as many weeks, news helicopters hovered as crews worked to capture a glimpse of the well-attended affair.

Samson, Paulo and Lugo stood stoically near the casket, each working to put on the face of bravery for the hundreds of pairs of eyes on them. Anyone looking, however, could see the shadows of beards and the drawn tightness of their handsomely crafted features. The brothers hadn't had an easy time of maintaining their emotions.

Khouri and Setha had returned that morning from honeymooning in the Virgin Islands. No one knew how best to approach Danilo Melendez's only daughter, who stood just as stoically as her husband.

The eulogy ended with prayer and then the singing of Dan's late wife's favorite hymn, "Blessed Assurance." Crying and individual words of praise could be heard among the singing.

Khouri squeezed his wife's hand until she looked up at him. He kissed the corner of her eye.

"I've been told my shoulder's a good one to cry on." As he hoped, a smile forced its way to Setha's dark, lovely face.

The gesture faded, and in moments, the tears she'd suppressed funneled through in a wave as she cried against Khouri's broad shoulder.

During the mingling at the close of the service, Basil met up with Lucas Anton and the two men spoke over the surprise of Danilo's passing after so much happiness.

"Wasn't all happiness." Luc regarded the solemn scene with a mix of keen interest and melancholy. "Stress of it all probably weighed too heavy on Dan and his heart couldn't stand it."

"Did he talk about anything during those last days?" Basil regarded his old acquaintance pensively.

Luc frowned. "Such as?"

"People often want to confide when they feel the end is near."

"Basil." Luc shook his head while running a hand through the salt-and-pepper hair he'd acquired prematurely. "I doubt he thought the end was near. The attack was sudden, wasn't it?"

"I don't mean that, Luc. These murders…" Basil stepped closer to Luc. "They weighed on Dan heavy and not because the victims were MM employees."

"I don't know what you're getting at, Bas."

"Dan knew. He knew there was a chance this was all connected."

Luc gave up on trying to fake an easy expression. "That was a long time ago."

"Not so long ago." Basil regarded the crowd blandly. "Dan knew it was still going on. I turned my back on it, but even I knew. I told him to get out of it. I told him that all the time." He ground his jaw on a vicious curse. "I knew one day it'd come back to bite us all."

"And where has it bitten you? You haven't unexpectedly lost any employees?" Luc snapped and froze a second later as he recollected Wade Cornelius's death.

"I'm sorry, Basil." Again Luc shook his head. "I know Wade was a good friend to you. But you're letting Dan's death get to you. That's where this is coming from."

"He came to me. Wade. The day he quit. We argued... He'd discovered something or at least he *thought* it was something about John Holloway's suicide."

Luc blinked.

"Wade said he'd gotten it wrong, that he was meeting with Vita Holloway to get more facts." Basil rubbed his forehead. "He told me my...*friend* Melendez wasn't as lily-white as we'd been portraying him all those years. Hell, I knew that." Basil bit out the words in anger but quickly reverted back to despair. "To reveal Dan was to reveal myself and my part in the whole thing."

"Bas—"

"I fired him, Luc." Basil's anger had returned, glinting in his hazel eyes. "I lost my oldest friend in the process and waited too many years to tell him. I'm sorry—now he's dead."

"Have the police confirmed Wade's death was tied to MM?"

"Hell, Luc, the man signed his death warrant the minute he decided to write that book of his. You remember that, don't you?"

"Basil." Lucas raised his hands slowly, defensively. "Now, this is not time to be having a crisis of conscience."

"I think it's a perfect time."

"Anyone involved in all that mess is either dead or dying. Let it go."

"Luc, you're forgetting that there's someone out

there who obviously hasn't *let it go*. Innocent people
are being killed—"

"They weren't so innocent!"

The outburst gave Basil pause.

"Dan is dead. Let this die with him. There's been
enough bloodshed."

Basil remained silent, watching as Luc disappeared
into the crowd.

Avra was massaging the arch of her foot, taking a
break from the crowd, the sadness and the speculation.
She was filled with sorrow over the family's loss but
was relieved it hadn't been linked to another murder.
Neither family could withstand another blow.

She gave a start at rustling among the tall bushes
that sheltered her hiding place.

"Sorry," Sam said when he showed himself.

Avra laughed softly when he joined her on the stone
bench and assumed the job of massaging her foot.

"Is it that bad that you'd rather give me a foot massage?" she teased, hoping to lighten the mood in any
way that she could.

Sam didn't veer from the task. "It's *that* bad."

"How are you?" she asked once they'd managed to
share brief laughter.

"Terrible," he blurted with a slow shake of his dark
head. "Only two things will help. To solve this crime
and to have you back."

Avra blinked and knew her gaze had gone dreamy.

Sam didn't appear to notice. "We solved the map,"
he said and focused on her arch. "Leads to Mexico."

"Mexico."

"Humph. Right in our own backyard."

"Sam, what is this?" Avra spoke around her thumb tapping her lip.

"I don't know, but I'm about to find out. Care to join me?"

Avra was opening her mouth to tell him yes.

Sam expected her refusal. "I leave tomorrow for the airstrip—same one as before. You remember?"

Memories of the Kemah trip came to mind as she nodded.

Sam squeezed her foot. "This good?"

"Mmm-hmm." She stepped into a black pump. "Thank you."

"I'll be out around 10:00 a.m." He didn't wait for her confirmation of denial, but kissed the corner of her mouth and left her as quietly as he'd arrived.

Chapter 16

The crew of the ML1 knew better than to question the plans or destinations of its employers. When one of the Melendezes requested a flight, the crew knew their job was to be ready without a second's hesitation.

Still, the crew of the private plane weren't so disciplined that they didn't discuss the motivations of their employers among themselves. Such was the case that morning. The plane was fueled, inspected and cleared for takeoff yet they remained in place on the airstrip at the orders of Samson Melendez. Finally, Captain Joshua Ransome took it upon himself to question his employer and friend.

"You sure she'll come?" Josh asked once Sam explained why they were waiting.

"I'm sure of it." Sam let his guard down for his friend. "She wants answers just as much as I do."

"Maybe she wants to find them on her own." Josh

tipped the cap back on his head and shrugged. "From what I've heard, Avra Ross is a lady who knows what she wants and gets it how she wants it."

"Amen to that." Sam chuckled the words. "Am I actin' like a fool?"

Josh grinned and clapped Sam's back. "You're allowed. It's one of the side effects."

A playful frown softened Sam's face. "Side effects of what?"

"Of being in love," Josh sang and then nodded past Sam's shoulder. "There's your girl." The captain waved toward a few of his crew members and directed them to assist Avra with her bags. He then clapped Sam's shoulder again and returned to the plane.

Sam watched her leaving the foreign-model crossover she'd driven to the strip. *When had it happened?* he asked himself, realizing he had to know the date and time that he discovered he loved her. Just then, however, his mind was a blank.

His bottomless eyes trailed her body, lingering for an exceptionally long while on her bottom swelling beneath the snug dark denims she wore. A curse rumbled somewhere in the back of his mind and he made an honest attempt to set it elsewhere. Sadly, it hadn't veered far from that subject over the past few weeks. It would do him even less good to dwell on it then, he realized.

Josh was right—Avra Ross got what she wanted *how* she wanted it. He'd been walking around in a haze, missing her and cursing himself for screwing up. Of course, he wasn't so far gone that he couldn't see that she still wanted him. Did she want more than the obvious? *That* he couldn't be sure of.

"Sorry, Sam." Avra approached in a huff, her expression truly apologetic. "Khouri's gone off on another trip with his wife." She smiled.

Sam grinned. "They deserve it." His voice sounded melancholy in spite of his grin. "How's your dad?"

"Not so good." Her smile over Khouri and Setha's trip began to fade. "Didn't come in this morning—didn't call."

Sam didn't like the sound of that, and it showed on the tightly drawn tinge to his attractive features.

Avra shook her head, easily reading his expression. "He's fine—physically Fiona looked in on him, took Rock with her." She referred to her sisters.

"Are you okay?" Sam reached out to run his fingers on the capped chiffon sleeves of her turquoise blouse.

She gave a quick toss of her curls. "A few fires to put out at Ross, which is why I'm late. I really am sorry—thanks for waiting."

"It's fine." He waved off her second apology knowing the words he spoke were the truth. All was well; he didn't feel nearly as anxious as he had.

"After you," he said and they boarded the plane.

"The first MM spots should show up in the *Review* within the next month or so," Avra announced later as they finished off the bagels and flavored coffee provided during the flight.

"Humph." Sam gestured while wiping his hands with a black linen napkin near his saucer.

"What's that for?" Avra questioned the gesture.

Sam allowed a smile to tug the curve of his lips. "I just never thought our *inability* to work together would result in…all this."

"Humph." Avra mimicked Sam's earlier gesture.

"I know Khouri and Setha sure are happier because of that."

"True—" Sam nodded "—but I was thinking about us."

"I know you signed the contract before we left for Kemah." Avra kept her gaze on the corner of bagel she'd left behind. "Why'd you do that?"

"Because it was the right thing to do."

"You made such a big thing about *not* doing it, though."

Sam leaned back in the swivel chair and regarded her unwaveringly. "Guess I was tryin' to give you what you expected of me." He winked when she met his gaze.

Avra laughed and then quieted as Sam's expression harbored a more somber aura. Leaning close, he reached across the short coffee table separating them and took her hand in his. "I never set out to destroy whatever trust you had or were starting to have in me." He rubbed her fingers between his.

"I know that, Sam."

His head snapped up. "You do?"

"I have to." She sighed.

"Why?"

"Howdy, folks." Josh Ransome's voice came across the speaker then. "We're about to land here, y'all, so buckle up tight. This one's gonna be bumpy."

Chihuahuan Desert, Mexico

The plane set down in the city of Chihuahua located within the desert that straddled the U.S. and Mexico border and was the third largest desert in the Western Hemisphere.

Sam's and Avra's things were taken to the hotel while they boarded a Jeep destined for the desert and the mysterious 14918 Figueroa Trail.

Josh rode up front with the driver and together they carried on conversation in a stream of Spanish. Sam kept Avra company in the back, but his gaze was fixed on the driver and his pilot w¿hile he followed their conversation.

"What are they saying?" Avra whispered. Despite the fact that her Spanish fluency was near perfect, there were aspects of certain dialects she didn't quite comprehend.

"The place has been abandoned," Sam whispered.

"He knows where it is?" Warily Avra surveyed the driver—a disheveled-looking man dressed in a worn shirt and gauchos with a matching cloth hat.

"Address is a fake," Sam added. "They just made it up to have a name to call it by."

"Why?"

Sam shook his head once. He was silent for a while until some part of the conversation piqued his interest.

"¿Que?" he asked.

"Está abandonado," the driver said.

Sam moved toward the edge of the seat. *"¿Cuándo?"*

"Tres meses, señor. *Más o menos."* The man's voice was barely audible.

Sam released a soft breath.

"What?" Avra slapped Sam's thigh when he took his time about filling her in.

"He says the place has been abandoned for at least three months."

She shuddered then and Sam reached for her hand. He wasn't surprised to find it cold even though they were in the middle of the desert. Squeezing tight, he tugged at it and kissed the back of it.

"Don't wimp out on me," he murmured into her skin. As he hoped, the taunt made her smile.

"Sam, I'm scared." She moved closer to him as if to absorb warmth. "You know we'll have to tell Brad Crest about whatever we find out here."

He kissed the back of her hand again. "We'll worry about it when we get there."

"How much farther is it?"

Sam moved toward the front seat to translate Avra's question to the driver.

"Ten minutes," he told her.

Avra clutched the tail of the burgundy chambray shirt that hung outside Sam's jeans. The Jeep had pulled to a stop before the house that, until then, she'd only seen in photos and on the wall in Samson's den.

She was first to leave the Jeep but took no steps closer to the construction. The soft leather hat she wore blew off her head and would have been lost to the desert were it not for the chin strap keeping it at her neck.

Sam set it back atop her head to protect her from the blaring sun. Then he cupped her elbow and led her along with him toward the house.

In addition to the house, they could see other buildings on the property. None of them were dilapidated or appeared in need of repair, however. The area may have been abandoned months before, but it had been used and well cared for up until that time. Sam and Avra went to explore one of the buildings—subconsciously avoiding the house that had plagued their thoughts.

The apprehension on Avra's face faded when she

looked through a window in the brick construction. Inside, the place had the appearance of a restaurant complete with tablecloths covering round tables already set for a meal.

The driver approached the entrance with a pair of bolt cutters and made quick work of breaking the chain binding the door. Once inside the dwelling, everyone's jaws dropped as the true luxury of the space was revealed. In addition to the dining area, there was what appeared to be a dance floor in the center of the room.

"Sam…" Avra looked up and around like a child in awe. "What is this?"

Sam could barely shake his head. He was thoroughly perplexed.

"I'll go unlock the house." Josh took the cutters from the driver.

Avra and Sam exchanged looks and then turned in unison and left on Josh's heels. Avra couldn't resist looking back at the restaurant-dancehall-warehouse. She was grateful when Sam took her arm again and pulled her alongside him.

The main building was an equally stunning piece of architecture. It was old but obviously well maintained and spacious. *Extremely* spacious. It seemed that the front of the house visible in the photos was merely a foyer. Basil Ross's earlier picture had only captured that portion. Or, Avra thought, perhaps that was all there had been back then.

"Sam…this is a mansion."

They crossed into the living room. It was a plushly furnished room complete with chandeliers and an impressive bar that spanned an entire wall.

"What's this kind of place doing in the middle of the desert?" Josh asked the driver in English.

The man understood. "I only know of the location, señor, as I said on the phone."

"You've been here." Sam's heavy voice rumbled. The words weren't phrased as a question.

The driver worried the frayed edges of his shirt-sleeve. "I have taken people here before, señor."

"What people?"

"Important ones, señor."

A sound caught Avra's ear and she turned her head, looking up at the ceiling. "Someone's here."

The men ran up the wide, curving staircase just outside the living room. Avra followed closely behind, stopping where the stairs branched off. For only a moment the group was stunned by the lavishness of the bedrooms lining the long corridors on either side of the landing.

Avra emerged the victor when she located the source of the noise in the first bedroom she entered. The woman there brandished a shard from the lamp she'd just broken.

"Sam!" Avra had her hands raised in a defensive pose.

He was bounding into the room seconds after her call.

Avra merely pointed and Sam's glare cleared when he saw the woman huddled in the corner.

"Está bien." Softly Sam cooed to the woman that all was well. He extended a hand slowly hoping to relay the truth in the statement. *"Está bien*...Josh?" His voice was firm yet gentle so as not to further terrify the cowering woman.

"Carla?" the driver blurted seconds after he and Josh ran into the room.

The woman blinked once owlishly and then again and still again more rapidly as recognition seemed to emerge.

"Juanito?"

"Carla..." Juanito rushed forward, stooping to his heels and gathering the woman to his chest. The words he whispered were barely audible, but Avra, Sam and Josh all comprehended when Juanito told Carla that he'd thought she was dead.

"What went on here, Juan?" Josh asked once the conversation between Juanito and Carla began to wane.

Juanito stood with Carla tucked tightly beneath the hollow of his arm. "Outside," he insisted.

"I wouldn't want to be in there any longer than *I* had to, either. Gorgeous but eerie," Avra noted with a shiver when they all stood near the Jeep.

Sam held Avra close, frequently dropping kisses to the top of her unruly hair. The closeness was for her reassurance as much as his.

"Please, Juan, what happened here?" Josh intruded softly on the intense conversation between Juanito and Carla that had lasted close to fifteen minutes.

"Parties happened here, señor." Juan's hold on Carla's small, round frame was clearly proprietary. "All the time parties. Rich people from America would come here for parties." Juan's dark gaze was fixed and hate-filled toward the mansion. "On this side of the border they paid the officials so the parties could be—how you say—unrestricted."

"Drugs," Josh guessed.

Juanito held his lips against Carla's brow for a time.

"She's worked here as a maid since she was twelve. Once she hoped to go into America for a 'new life.' It was the dream her mother had for her, but she was not pretty enough."

"Not pretty enough." Avra frowned.

"*Lo siento,* señorita," Juan apologized. "They are her words."

"What the hell's her looks got to do with her getting into the States?" Sam asked, frowning viciously at Juan.

"They all want to go to America. They come here first to work and earn their papers." Juan nodded slightly toward the house in the distance. "The rich people who come here for the parties could make that happen quickly."

"Why is the place deserted?"

Juan gave Avra a sad smile. "News from the States. Some of the people who worked here were killed—they are investigating. Carla says those in charge thought it best to close down for a while." Again he squeezed the small woman. "She had nowhere to go. She had overheard the talk—they sounded like it wouldn't be long so she hid inside. She ran out of food two weeks ago."

"You know each other."

Juan looked toward Sam, who had spoken. "When the rich people weren't here for their parties, the workers took care of the house. They lived here and could have parties of their own, señor. Everyone in town knew about the big house in the desert."

"How do you know about these rich people?" Josh asked.

"Carla just told me. I didn't know that's what they

came for. I always thought it was business for Señor Danilo. He lived here when he came to do work."

Avra looked up at Sam when his voice vibrated from his chest through her body.

"My father stayed here?" he'd asked.

Juan was nodding. "Everyone knew Señor Danilo had jobs across the border. Many came here for the chance to be hired and go there to work and be happy…" He patted Carla's hand when she curled one into his shirt. "The quality of their work determined their position in Señor Dan's company."

Avra bowed her head and began to fan her blouse away from her chest.

"The heat is murder," Josh grumbled, removing his cap to wipe a handkerchief across his brow. "Maybe it's time to head back." He looked to Sam for agreement.

"What about Carla?" Avra asked.

"She has friends in Chihuahua—she is very proud and would not go to them. They've been worried for her. I'll see that she gets to them."

"Thank you, Juanito."

The man bowed his head toward Avra and then helped Carla into the vehicle.

Avra felt Sam's hands at her shoulders next.

"Let's go, darlin'," he murmured against her cheek.

Avra cast one last look back at the house and then stepped up into the Jeep.

Chapter 17

After showers and naps in their respective rooms, Sam and Avra decided to meet down in the hotel restaurant. Avra got a slow start and then lost interest in eating altogether. Sam came knocking on her door twenty minutes after the time they had planned to meet.

At the door he easily read her expression and settled both hands on her shoulders. Applying a light massage there, he pressed his cheek to hers and smiled when she squeezed one of his hands.

"This can't be Avra Ross lookin' all defeated." He blurted out the tease, giving her slight frame an enthusiastic tug. "Why, I've heard she drinks fire and belches lightnin'!"

The words made her smile but not laugh as Sam had hoped.

"Come on, darlin'." He hid his handsome face in the crook of her neck. "It'll be all right."

"Will it?" She pulled back to look up at him and issue the challenge. "This is worse than we think, isn't it?"

"Shh…" He held her close then. Rising to his full height, he urged her to share a seat with him on the sofa in the living area.

"You think Carla didn't tell us everything?" he asked.

"I don't think we asked the right questions."

"Hell." Sam massaged his eyes then, allowing that much of his weariness to show. "I agree."

"And I can't stop wondering why those people were killed—everything tells me it had something to do with that damn house."

"Maybe someone saw something they weren't supposed to see." Avra tucked her nightshirt around her thighs and rested her head back on her palm. "Rich people partying…important people…"

"We're gonna have to talk to her again."

Avra agreed with Samson's groaned words. "We've come too far not to get the entire story." She took her turn at groaning then, tossing an arm over her eyes while falling back on the opposite side of the sofa.

Sam observed her guardedly and then muttered an unreadable curse. "Guess I'll be sayin' good-night." He prepared to stand.

"Don't go." She suddenly moved to her knees.

Sam allowed his enviably long lashes to drift down for just a moment.

"Sam?"

"Baby, I can't stay."

"Why not?"

"Dammit, Avra." A muscle flipped somersaults

along his jaw when it clenched. "Trying to solve this mystery might be enough to keep your thoughts occupied, but it ain't nearly enough to keep my mind off… other things."

Her heart lurched. Her thoughts were jerked clear back to *other things* when she saw the path his black stare charted down her body. She may have whispered his name but his mouth was on hers in seconds. Resistance was not relevant nor was it possible. She sighed his name in the midst of thrusting her tongue hungrily against his, seeking out the pressure of the kiss, relishing it.

"How long are you going to punish me, Av?" The words sounded tortured as he tugged her lobe between his perfect teeth and uttered them softly.

"I'm not punishing you, only…" She breathed in sharply when he tugged at both her arms in silent demand of her confession. "This scares me, Sam."

His hold weakened on her arms. "You're afraid of me?" The hurt in his voice was unmistakable.

Avra shook her head, moving against the arm of the sofa when he released her. "Sam, there's a reason why I'm alone." She fixed him with a sad smile. "I can be very hard to take, as you well know." Her smile turned rueful. "Men say they like strength in a woman but I don't think they mean it. The men I've…let get close certainly haven't liked it very much."

"Then the men you've let get close have been idiots." Sam shook his head and then studied the hand he repeatedly flexed into a fist. "You know I'm not like that and you're lying to yourself if you think otherwise."

"Sam—"

"Shut up. I'm in love with you."

She wilted. "Sam…"

"Deny it," he demanded, pulling her next to him, which forced her to look into his eyes. "Deny that you feel that way about me, Avra?"

"I can't." She swiped a tear escaping the corner of her eye. "I love you."

Sam bowed his head for a moment, savoring the sound of the words he felt he'd waited an eternity to hear. Eventually he looked up at her in confusion. "Then, Avra, why—"

"What if I mess us up, Sam?" Her vivid gaze was pleading. "I'm not like the women you date."

He smiled, his bottomless gaze crinkling adorably. "How do you know about the women I date?"

"*Please,* you and your brothers are among Houston's most eligible. Women talk and I know that your taste tends to run toward the slutty and stupid."

"True." He accepted the assessment with barely a shrug. "And it was actually good enough till you tornadoed into my life."

"You're used to women obeying because they want to please you, get a key to that gorgeous ranch and put their slippers under your bed." She pulled her fingers through her hair and then hugged her knees to her chest. "I don't know how to do that, Sam. Not even for the man I love."

Agitation stirred in the ebony depths of his stare. "You're a fool if you think I'd ever want you to be that."

"You say that now." Her smile had an air of sympathy. "I've never really loved a man in the romantic sense. Maybe what I'm really afraid of is losing myself if we don't make it."

"Darlin'…" Sam moved, brushing his lips across

her cheeks to capture the tears appearing there. The gesture hovered near her mouth but he broke the kiss before she could participate.

"Do you love me enough to risk it?" His mouth was trailing her jaw then.

"Samson—"

As if he sensed argument on her lips, he kissed her again to swallow her words. This kiss was much more heated, wetter and held Avra suspended in fascination and helpless to do more than lazily entwine her tongue around his once she was in his lap.

A shiver kissed her skin and she realized she was bare. Slowly and with the finesse of an expert, Sam had relieved her of the cotton nightshirt. Hand on her thigh, he dragged her beneath him on the sofa, which was far too short for their tall frames. It served its purpose for a time.

Lightly his mouth skimmed the curve of her breasts, her rib cage and hip. He tongued her navel without mercy and held her arms captive at her sides when she wriggled in response to being both pleasured and tickled by the whiskers on his face.

"Do you love me enough to risk it?" he growled into her abdomen.

Avra however was too far gone to speak. Apology flew to her lips when he suddenly pulled her off the sofa. She realized it was to take her to the queen-size bed in the back. The brief trip was as much time as he allowed her to acknowledge the change in location. His mouth was fusing to her skin once more, easing lower along her body. He nibbled the inside of her thighs. He used his nose to nudge and outline the bare, triangular patch of skin above her sex.

When Sam released Avra's arms, she sank her hands into his hair. Insistently she arched her hips to encourage him to put his tongue inside her. Sam ignored that plea, even when she whimpered in the most ego-stroking fashion and nudged her hip against his jaw. He only tortured her more, barely skimming his mouth across her feminine folds.

"Mmm…Sam…"

"Do you love me enough to risk it, babe?"

"Sam, I—"

Still, he wasn't satisfied with the manner she began her response. He raised himself over her, tugged her from her back and subjected her to another stirring kiss.

Avra locked her arms about his neck and rubbed her nipples into the rough fabric of his shirt. That only lasted until Sam planted his hand on the center of her back and crushed her breasts into his chest. Her seductive kiss shifted into one of desperation and loss over the sensation of his touch. She smoothed her bare legs along the length of his trouser-covered ones and then locked them behind his back and ground herself against him. She pushed her hands up along the powerful wall of his chest, curving her fingers into his shirt before tugging it apart to reveal his sleek, dark copper skin.

She broke the kiss that time and used her teeth to graze and bite the cords lining his neck. Flicking rounded thumbnails across his nipples, she followed the gesture with an intense suckling.

"Avra." Sam relaxed on the bed, happy to relinquish the lead.

Avra followed him down to the tangled queen-size, grinding and moaning while she suckled and squeezed his nipples. Mercilessly her fingers worked over the other. Sam was desperate then, as well, to get out of his clothes and into her.

Hungrily, she feasted on his torso as he came out of the shirt. She tasted every stunning inch of skin bared. With the tip of her tongue she charted a breathtaking path across the array of muscles packed into his abdomen. Sam clutched her bottom and drew her up high to kiss him then. He kept her cradled in one hand while the other went to work on his trouser fastening.

Avra was deep in the midst of another mind-altering kiss. She only pulled her mouth from his to move higher against him and replace her mouth with her breast.

Sam was enthusiastic in his handling of her breast. He outlined the pert plumpness with his nose and then his tongue returned to the diamond-hard nipple. Meanwhile, he applied the condom he'd pulled from his pocket before kicking off his boots, socks and trousers. He took her hips and settled her sweetly— suddenly—to his wide, lengthy erection.

Another wave of sensation had Avra convulsing deliciously as the force of it welled inside her. Cupping her breasts, she rolled her hips vigorously and shamelessly cried out while tossing back her head. Her own pleasure was uppermost in her mind while she rode Sam's glorious stiffness in search of her release. When he pulled her off, she could have hit him.

He resumed control, ravenously licking and outlining her nipples. He reclaimed her body. A hand imprisoned each of her thighs and he spread her to his satisfaction all the while increasing the power behind his thrusts.

Avra had no strength in her hands but she did her

best to hold on to Sam's massive forearms. She did, however, meet his forceful lunges with a fire of her own. Sam was on the brink of eruption. The sight of Avra's breasts bouncing and beckoning, her tight, wet heat gloving him and her airy cries as she took him pushed him well over the cliff of splendid madness.

The volume of sound in the room was courtesy of breathy moans and curses of approval. Sam rolled to his back suddenly and took Avra with him. There, he cuffed his hand about her neck.

"Do you love me enough to risk it, Avra?"

"Yes, Sam." There was no hesitation and her eyes reflected sincerity. "Yes, I love you. I damn well love you enough to risk it."

The next afternoon Avra was asking Sam to translate their appreciation to Carla Jiminez for agreeing to see them again. The woman looked almost miniscule in the green recliner that sat majestically in the corner of her friend's living room.

"I speak English, señora." Carla's voice was small like her stature. "Señor Dan made sure everyone who worked at the house could." She looked to Sam. "He was your father, yes?" Her lips thinned as if to smile. "You look like he did all those years ago, but bigger." She lowered her gaze demurely.

Sam smiled. "He passed on recently," he shared.

Carla nodded. "Juanito told me. I'm sorry for your loss."

Silently Avra noted that the words didn't ring true in the woman's dark eyes. "Carla, do you know what's happening in the States? The murders? Did the workers at the house see anything? Overhear anything that might have put them in danger?"

Carla was already shaking her head defiantly. "Not what they saw. What they did."

Avra nudged Sam's knee with hers as they sat close on the sofa facing the recliner. The gesture offered a measure of the reassurance she needed but didn't believe it was possible to attain.

"The pretty ones went to the parties with Señor Dan's friends—the upstairs bedrooms were theirs. They didn't have to clean." Carla expelled the breath she'd held while the confession whooshed out.

"They were sleeping with them." Avra leaned over to brace her elbows on her knees.

"My father used them as prostitutes—it's how they…" Sam followed Avra's gesture and was soon leaning over, as well. "It was how they earned their way into the country." He covered his face in his hands.

Avra couldn't sit still and began to walk the small room.

"Señor Luc always talked to us about leaving."

Carla's small voice ceased Avra's pacing. Sam straightened.

"Luc? Anton?" Avra queried.

"He came down often. Sometimes when Señor Dan was there we could hear them arguing." Carla's stiff pose showed signs of softening as she shared more of the story. "Some did stop, but only because they married well."

"Vita Arroyo," Avra guessed.

Carla smiled, her round face beaming at the memory of the woman. "She was one of them. Cute boys she had with Señor John…"

"She was Señor Luc's favorite." Carla looked to Sam. "When she married, he was very happy for her and used her life as an example to the rest of us to get married and have real lives." She blinked and studied her hands clenched tightly then in her lap.

"But what Señor Dan offered was too great not to try for. To do anything for, even—even die for." She fixed Sam with a pitiful smile.

"I never wanted you to know this." Basil kept his back turned while speaking to the two couples who stood in his living room that night. After a lengthy span of silence he faced Khouri, Setha, Sam and Avra.

"Dan and I never wanted *any* of you to know. We never planned it—it just…just happened." He seemed bewildered, conjuring the memory of the time.

"We got the idea one night after we all visited a parlor for drinks—me, Dan, Luc, Russ Otis… At first it was all in fun, talkin' big and stupid. We were so young." Sadness dimmed his gaze.

"Next thing I know, Dan's showin' me the spot where he wants to build the damn place… We started small." He went to stand before the bay windows at the back of the room. "That shack was all we could afford at first. But it was enough and it didn't take long for us to be seduced by the money. We convinced ourselves that everybody was getting what they wanted. We knew that was a lie." He braced his hands on the windows and curled them into fists. "We had them sign papers promising they wouldn't discuss it.

"I'm sorry." He gushed the words and hung his head low. "I know that's not nearly enough. When we became family men…when I had daughters of my own…"

He looked toward Avra. "I felt sick being a part of it—you all would've grown up together had I not been determined to erase that part of my life, to act like it never existed. I talked to Dan…so many times I talked to him about making it right. Humph, makin' it right…" He took his hands from the windows and hugged himself. "He'd lived the lie so long—he didn't know how to end it much less make up for it. Make it right…" He closed his eyes.

Avra crossed the room to her father. "Daddy…" She eased her arms about his waist and smiled when he clutched her hand. "I think I may know a way." She spoke across his shoulder.

"What way?" Khouri asked as he, Setha and Sam moved closer.

Avra turned to face them. "We're gonna need our notes."

Detective Bradley Crest was on his way out the back door while trying to gobble down the last of his coffee and breakfast.

"Leavin', Cess!" he called out to his wife.

"Hold up, darlin'!" Cecily Crest's blond waist-length locks brushed her back as she rushed into the kitchen carrying a package. "I just signed for this." She was breathless.

Brad tossed down a napkin and reached for the package and opened it without ceremony. There was a smaller box inside the larger outer one. Blinking, Brad took a closer look at the labeling.

"What's wrong, sugar?" Cecily inquired of the look on her husband's rugged face.

Brad only shook his head and pulled Cecily close for a kiss. "I may be late," he told her.

While Brad Crest made his way in to work that morning, households across Houston were abuzz with talk of that day's *Ross Review* and the front-page story that had the potential to ruin it.

Entrepreneurs Linked to Prostitution in Mexico

Avra's idea to be first in airing the Ross and Melendez dirty laundry was agreed upon by the members of both families. As she stood in Sam's kitchen that morning and read the story, Avra prayed they had made the right decision.

As though receiving an answer to her prayer, Sam's arms encircled her waist then.

"Did we do the right thing, Sam?" She pressed her hand to the side of his face when he kissed her neck.

"We did the best thing." His words were deep, reassuring and muffled against her skin. "It was past time for all this mess to come out."

"Even if I pissed away our inheritances in the process?" She smiled, feeling chuckles shake his big frame.

"Well, now...seein' as I've already gone and fallen in love with you..."

They shared brief laughter and drew strength from one another as their embrace tightened.

Sam applied a similar kiss to the other side of Avra's neck. "Will you believe me if I tell you it'll be all right?"

Avra let her eyes drift closed and relished the security of his arms around her. "I'd believe you." She sighed the words.

Sam eased his hands beneath the short silk robe she wore. Avra had stayed with him since they had returned from Mexico almost a week earlier.

His fingers drifted down her abdomen to play and the wicked lunges and rotations had her weak for more. With his unoccupied hand he cupped her chin to angle her for a deep kiss even as his fingers played below and probed with greater insistence. Lazily Avra pushed her tongue against his, relishing the slow ooze of need coursing through her like honey. She curved her hands over the counter and absorbed wave upon wave of sensation stemming from his thrusts.

Sam moved his hand from her chin to her breast and squeezed possessively before assaulting a nipple until it firmed between his thumb and index.

She tried to moan his name, but only a mixed garble of sound wafted from her throat. Boldly she clutched his wrist as silent encouragement that he deepen his penetration. When she uttered what resembled a curse, he laughed softly and questioned the outburst.

"We should be upstairs…"

"What for?" Understanding her frustration, he produced a condom from the front pocket of the denim shorts he'd tugged on to come find her.

Avra's anticipation was evident in the shivers claiming her when she heard Sam's shorts hit the kitchen floor with a soft swish. She raised her arms, reaching up and back to wind them about his neck. Toying in his glossy, dark crop of hair, she wanted to sob her pleasure when his sex claimed hers. At once his erect endowment was soaking in an abundance of the moisture he'd coaxed from her core.

Sam hooked a hand about her thigh, raising it and subsequently deepening his penetration if that were possible. Avra cried his name loud and clear that time. The sound had him increasing the speed of his drives inside her.

Perfect teeth grazed the satiny, dark column of her neck, and Sam clutched the countertop, as well, forcing her to bend more to his will. He growled a curse and stripped her of the robe, which barely clung to her back. He kicked away the shorts pooled at his feet and then withdrew in order to lift her high and settled her on the countertop. The move sent pleasure rippling through her.

"Sam, no..." Avra could feel his rock-solidness stiffen more intensely then in the telltale fashion, signifying the approach of his climax.

Samson ignored her pleas, preferring to give in to the roar of his hormones. He kept her close, smiling when she beat a fist on his shoulder.

Avra shrieked when he slapped her bottom in retaliation. Next he was hoisting her across the shoulder she'd subjected to a pounding fist moments earlier.

"Don't worry." He bit into a lush portion of her thigh. "I'm not done yet."

Chapter 18

The Melendez Rodeo was an annual event first organized as a marketing event when Sam obtained a job in his father's company. Over the years the rodeo had transformed from a marketing affair to a charity gala. Tickets started at $5,000, $10,000 for those wanting to sponsor one of the bull riders or horse wranglers.

Whatever worries there may have been over fallout from the story, they were moot at that point. The event boasted its largest gross in years. It went without saying that those in attendance were impressed by the guts shown by the families to own up to the darkness in their pasts.

"Anybody could happen along here, you know?" Avra's voice seemed to echo amid the movement of the tree leaves. She and Sam indulged in time alone near the large man-made pond along the rear of his property.

Sam continued his inspection of the mound of soft

flesh visible past the cups of the lacy baby-blue bra Avra wore beneath a navy shirt. The buttons were almost completely undone.

"Guess we should give 'em a good show, then, huh?"

Avra rolled her eyes but couldn't fight the smile that tugged her mouth. The desire to laugh was triggered by more than finding humor in Sam's words. The honesty they had enjoyed in Mexico had not been a singular occurrence.

Avra never expected she of all people could be so free with sharing the things she had with Sam over the past several days. Even her concerns about whether they would last seemed to have taken a backseat—*no* seat if truth be told. She was content—utterly so—to enjoy the delight of his company and hope that it would linger. Thoughts of it ending held no sway over her emotions then.

Sam appeared to reside on a plane of equal happiness. He, however, wasn't as eager to accept things as they were. He wanted more. He wanted all of Avra. He wanted her in every way—physically...well...that went without saying. There was more that he craved, though. He knew she was still plagued by fears of them not lasting. Such fears were understandable. Yet love was also in play and it was in *that* emotion he put his stock.

"Sam? Sam, you're not undoing my blouse."

"You're right, I'm not." He hid his face in her cleavage. "I already have."

His muffled voice vibrating into her skin pushed Avra into the laughter she'd been gradually giving in to anyway. Tunneling her fingers into his thick hair, she sighed contentedly while savoring the appearance of blue sky and white clouds above. Wisps of green from the treetops rounded out the spectacular view.

"We should take another trip." Sam's muffled voice resumed again.

Avra let her lashes drift down over her eyes. "Kemah?" she breathed.

"Maybe…but not for business."

"Mmm…I'm liking the sound of that more and more. Not that we took care of much *business* when we were there, you know?"

"Right." The reminder prompted Sam to lift his head. He kept close to Avra, trailing his fingers across her collarbone.

He applied the strokes absently but they produced distinct shivers throughout Avra's body nonetheless.

"What?" She questioned his set expression then.

Sam offered a halfhearted smile and shrug. "Trip I've got in mind would be a lot different from that. If I have my way…"

Avra's brows drew near as she tried to unravel the meaning of his words. "Why, Samson Melendez, don't you always get your way?"

Sam's smile did little to solve the mystery. "That remains to be seen, Ms. Ross" was all that he would say.

The vagueness was all a little too much for Avra then. She propped up on her elbows. "Sam, what—?"

"So everything's still okay at the magazine?"

Avra relaxed on her back and took no offence to his interruption. Snuggling into the soft grass, she smiled. "Surprisingly okay. I thought for sure we'd have some backlash in circulation, but nothing." She trailed her fingers up along the muscular width of his forearm. "Could be the calm before the storm," she noted.

"If so, then it's spread to my neck of the woods, too."

Avra angled her head. "All is well?" She sounded doubtful.

Sam shrugged. "As well as can be, I guess. I think it'll be a long time before anyone who works for MM really believes this is over."

"Yeah." Avra bit her lip on the thought. "I suppose a strong business has nothing on a content mind."

Sam merely allowed his lashes to shield his eyes briefly to confirm the truth of her words. "So are you sorry that your brother's officially tied you to my family?" he asked once the melody of wind, birds and trees had filled the air for a time.

"Ha! I can think of worse families to be part of." She sighed the words that were meant to be a tease.

Sam didn't appear to relish the humor of the phrase. The earlier set to his provocative copper-kissed features had returned. Avra knew it would be futile to attempt coaxing him to share whatever had him preoccupied.

She took comfort in the fact that his expression didn't appear harsh or even mildly agitated. He had the look of a man working to come to terms with something he was contemplating. Avra could only hope he'd share his conclusions once he'd settled the issue. In the meantime she decided it'd be best and far more enjoyable to direct her talents on putting him at ease.

"I can't believe you're here lookin' like a rain cloud

when you've got me on the ground and at your mercy." She waited to see if he'd rise to her playful challenge.

His resulting grin told her that her plan had succeeded.

Associates of Basil Ross and Danilo Melendez were understandably absent from the gathering. No one wanted to risk being suspected of having taken part in "The Matter" in Mexico. No one, as yet, had been arrested for the murders. Basil decided it was time for that mystery to be solved.

"Thanks for meeting me." Basil walked to the middle of the living room at Sam's ranch with his hand outstretched. "Surprised to see you show when so many of our friends didn't."

Luc Anton removed the charcoal-gray cowboy hat he wore and smiled at the sounds of the gala going on outside the house. "It's still an impressive event, but more for the younger set now." He sighed and set the hat on the back of a sofa. "We've become our fathers, Bas."

"Our fathers never dealt in our kind of business, Luc." Basil took a seat on the arm of the sofa. "It was you all along, wasn't it?"

Luc's easy expression showed faint traces of tightening.

"The murder victims were all the ones used for the prostitution end, weren't they? What was it, Luc? Were you afraid they'd talk? Why single *them* out? Why not the entire line? Or was it because they *wouldn't* talk?" Basil's eye was keen, his mind quick, and he made short work of calculating Luc's bristling.

"That's it. You wanted them to come out against

Dan, didn't you? But they wouldn't. Then you brought that poor girl's boys into it."

Basil's mention of Vita Arroyo's sons was the breaking point for Lucas.

"Dan was greedy!" His face reddened. "He should've shut that dirty business down a long time ago. I begged him. *You* begged him. You turned your back on him for years because of it. I told him that this would bury us one day."

"And you had those kids killed."

"Dan corrupted them with money and position." Luc waved his hand as if to reason away his culpability. "Someone had to say enough, otherwise it never would have ended."

"Dammit, Luc, it wasn't their burden to bear!"

"Bas, they weren't innocent kids anymore! We've all had to pay." Lucas's voice ended in a hissing whisper.

Basil's lip curled. "And they had to pay with their lives."

Luc shrugged and walked by the sofa to pick up his hat and then he set it back down again. "I couldn't risk them running to Dan and ruining…"

"What?"

Luc grimaced. "He was supposed to step down." His eyes blazed with fury and frustration. "He was so damned…stubborn."

Basil left the sofa, frowning with sudden understanding. "It was all about MM. You didn't give a damn about shutting this down. You wanted his company?"

"*His* company? The bastard didn't build it by himself, Bas. Staffing it with former prostitutes—educated or not—was going to turn out badly for us sooner or later."

"Evil bastard." Basil worked his fingers into his brow. "Why'd you bring those boys into it? What was in it for Holloway's sons?"

"Aw, they wanted revenge and rightfully so." Luc clenched a fist and shook it in Basil's direction. "Dan prostituted their mother and had their father killed when he threatened to pull the wool off the whole thing." Luc straightened then, detecting Basil's surprise. "You never knew... Yes, my friend, Dan definitely had that killer instinct. It was the same with Wade Cornelius. The fool actually wanted to put what he suspected into a book."

"Humph." Luc paced the room. "Then there was Carson. Hell, he was an angry buck! He wanted to kill *all* Dan's kids. Show him what it felt like to lose someone you love. He went after Setha. She was Dan's prize, his princess. But he was ready to kill anyone who had a hand in this. Unfortunately he was too much of a wild card to take care of Martin Viejo. The information Martin had could have brought us all down too fast. I had Tad take care of him, though." He sighed while referencing his henchman, Tad Filmon.

"He wasn't as much of a monster as you think, Luc." Basil shook his head on the man's confidence. "He gave my daughter-in-law the information she needed to start uncovering all this mess. Whether he meant to or not, he gave her the information needed to track all this back to you."

"Then he was angry *and* stupid." Luc tried to smile, intent on maintaining confidence, but he failed. "Whatever the case, I could only use him for a couple of the *immigrant murders*." He curved both pairs of index and middle fingers to form mock quotations. "The kid wasn't the smartest assassin."

"You're a monster."

Luc took no offense to the accusation. "Don't worry, Bas. You won't have long to torture yourself with the knowledge of all this." He nodded toward a tall, slender man who had emerged in the living-room doorway.

"It'll be quick," Luc promised when Basil looked at the man and then back to him. "I've always loved Sam's home—so many remote areas." He spread his arms. "Thanks for selecting the venue."

Luc's accomplice entered, closed and locked the door behind himself.

"Everyone will understand that you just couldn't live with the shame of what you and Dan did," Luc explained. "As for me, I'll be hard at work trying to clean up things at MM."

"Idiot," Basil almost snarled. "Have you already forgotten the man's three sons? Big ones with brains to match."

"Well, man, there're ways to handle brains…and brawn."

"Yes, there are…" Basil looked over at Luc's henchman, who was adding a silencing device to the gun he brandished. "Do you have what you need?"

Lucas was frowning over the question when the rumble of footsteps drew close to the door. In minutes Brad Crest and his men were crashing in, guns aimed and cocked.

"All right there, Mr. Ross?" Brad queried.

"Better now." Basil's grin portrayed relief. He loosened his collar and turned it so that Lucas could see the wire.

"Filthy rat," Luc breathed.

"Ah, cheer up, Mr. Anton," Brad urged. "You wanted everybody to own up to the past, right? That's all Mr. Ross was tryin' to do. Thanks to Shane Arroyo and a neat li'l package he asked his mother to forward in the event of his death, we can tie you to his murder. With any luck, Mr. Ross's efforts will tie you to the rest." Brad read Luc's questioning expression.

"Oh! Let me explain. Shane Arroyo was recording the part he played—the part you hired him to play. Thankfully he had the foresight to ship his damning package before he was killed. It's very revealing stuff. Fascinating, in fact… I haven't been able to tear myself away since I got it over a week ago."

"You've got nothing." Luc sneered even as he was handcuffed and read his rights. "My lawyers will have me home in time for breakfast."

The man's carefree attitude broke what little power Basil held over restraining his temper. He pushed through three of the towering officers and caught Lucas by his jacket lapels. "You would've killed him! You would've killed Dan, too, if the heart attack hadn't done it first!"

Lucas didn't answer. He didn't need to. The cool stare and faint smile he wore were answer enough.

Basil released him. Utter disbelief threw his dark face into further shadow when he stepped back to study Lucas Anton.

Soon after, Luc and his associate, Tad Filmon, were being led from the room.

A softly seductive guitar piece filtered in through the speakers in each corner of the bedroom. The rodeo had been a rousing success with promises of a more spectacular show next year. Sam and Avra left the cleaning to the hired crew and caterers, and they disappeared upstairs, where they collapsed onto the long sofa across from the bed. There, they dozed lightly off and on.

"Bravo…" Avra murmured, nuzzling her face into the crook of Sam's neck.

He kept his eyes closed. "What for?"

"Turning over the proceeds from the rodeo to the charities Martino Viejo scammed. Bravo."

"Guess he felt like it was owed to him. Can't say I blame him for thinking that." Sam spoke the words into the fragrant cloud of Avra's black curls and tugged her in closer to him. "Gonna take a lot more to make this right, though."

Avra shuddered. "I wish that Daddy would call…"

"Shh…don't worry. I'm guessing his statement will take a few hours, maybe more."

Avra squeezed her eyes closed. "What if they decide to arrest him afterward?"

"Don't think like that."

"But what if they do?"

"They won't."

"How do you know?"

Sam opened his eyes then and tugged Avra directly over him in order to look into her coffee-brown stare.

"Your dad's part in this ended a long time ago. The cops and the D.A. know that and will take it into consideration. Then there's the fact that he cooperated in bringing down Anton." His lashes fluttered, and he muttered a curse in reference to Luc Anton.

"I'm sorry, Sam." Avra skimmed her lips across his jaw. "I know how close he was to your dad."

"I guess you never really know anyone."

Avra was following the path her thumb made around Sam's seductive mouth. "I hope that's not true." She bit her lip when Sam's hands moved to cup her bottom through the snug-fitting jeans she sported. He cradled her into his firming sex and they shared a kiss.

"Okay." Avra gave an obedient nod when she pulled back. "You're right, the cops will take it into consideration. Everything will be fine."

He tweaked her chin. "That's my girl." Nuzzling her ear, he nibbled the lobe just slightly. "If what Brad says is true, Mr. B will be back home very soon."

Avra's frown was curious and playful. "What'd he say?"

Sam caressed her collarbone with his lips. "That my bride was gonna need someone to walk her down the aisle."

She blinked disbelief in her warm gaze.

"That is—" Sam winced a little "—if I can convince you to change your last name, Ms. Ross?"

Her lips parted and her stare reflected a knowing light. "Is this what you wouldn't say out at the pond?"

He shrugged. "I know there are worse families, but now mine is more scandalous than it ever was."

Avra's expression reflected regret. "I shouldn't have said that."

Sam tapped her bottom again while nudging her closer to his chest. "I'll forgive you for trashing my family, so long as you agree to become part of it."

Her smile was a mix of awe and excitement. "Why, Samson, are you asking me to be your Delilah?"

There was no playfulness on his set expression. "I love you, Avra. I'm asking you to be my wife. Do you love me enough to risk it?"

"I love you, Sam." Avra pressed her forehead to his. "I love you more than enough."

* * * * *

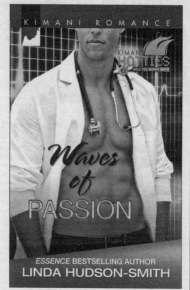

REQUEST YOUR FREE BOOKS!

2 FREE NOVELS
PLUS 2 FREE GIFTS!

KIMANI™
ROMANCE

Love's ultimate destination!

YES! Please send me 2 FREE Kimani™ Romance novels and my 2 FREE gifts (gifts are worth about $10). After receiving them, if I don't wish to receive any more books, I can return the shipping statement marked "cancel." If I don't cancel, I will receive 4 brand-new novels every month and be billed just $4.94 per book in the U.S. or $5.49 per book in Canada. That's a saving of at least 21% off the cover price. It's quite a bargain! Shipping and handling is just 50¢ per book in the U.S. and 75¢ per book in Canada.* I understand that accepting the 2 free books and gifts places me under no obligation to buy anything. I can always return a shipment and cancel at any time. Even if I never buy another book, the two free books and gifts are mine to keep forever.

168/368 XDN FEJR

Name	(PLEASE PRINT)
Address	Apt. #
City	State/Prov. Zip/Postal Code

Signature (if under 18, a parent or guardian must sign)

Mail to the **Reader Service:**
IN U.S.A.: P.O. Box 1867, Buffalo, NY 14240-1867
IN CANADA: P.O. Box 609, Fort Erie, Ontario L2A 5X3

Not valid for current subscribers to Kimani Romance books.

Want to try two free books from another line?
Call 1-800-873-8635 or visit www.ReaderService.com.

* Terms and prices subject to change without notice. Prices do not include applicable taxes. Sales tax applicable in N.Y. Canadian residents will be charged applicable taxes. Offer not valid in Quebec. This offer is limited to one order per household. All orders subject to credit approval. Credit or debit balances in a customer's account(s) may be offset by any other outstanding balance owed by or to the customer. Please allow 4 to 6 weeks for delivery. Offer available while quantities last.

Your Privacy—The Reader Service is committed to protecting your privacy. Our Privacy Policy is available online at www.ReaderService.com or upon request from the Reader Service.

We make a portion of our mailing list available to reputable third parties that offer products we believe may interest you. If you prefer that we not exchange your name with third parties, or if you wish to clarify or modify your communication preferences, please visit us at www.ReaderService.com/consumerschoice or write to us at Reader Service Preference Service, P.O. Box 9062, Buffalo, NY 14269. Include your complete name and address.

KROM11B

Two classic Westmoreland novels in one volume!

NEW YORK TIMES BESTSELLING AUTHOR

BRENDA JACKSON

DREAMS OF FOREVER

In *Seduction, Westmoreland Style,* Montana horse breeder McKinnon Quinn is adamant about his "no women on my ranch" rule…but Casey Westmoreland makes it very tempting to break the rules.

Spencer's Forbidden Passion has millionaire Spencer Westmoreland and Chardonnay Russell entering a marriage of convenience… but Chardonnay wants what is strictly forbidden.

"Sexy and sizzling." —*Library Journal* on *Intimate Seduction*

Available July 2012 wherever books are sold.

HARLEQUIN®
www.Harlequin.com

KPBJ4760712R